Now she couldn't mistake his smile. It curled his beautiful mouth deep at the corners. "In that department I can't speak for Dr. Stemmer. Only myself."

The Clayworth confidence *and* the Clayworth reputation with women set her on fire. She thrust up her chin. "*Probably* I've had my head up more skirts than you. Vintage ones for sure!"

"That's debatable," he muttered, lowering his lids for an instant over those cornflower eyes.

"Of course, how could I possibly have forgotten?" she drawled, helpless not to. "I remember the item Rebecca ran about you and your cousins closing down a restaurant in Paris while cavorting with a troupe of topless can-can dancers."

His lips twitched and his eyes lightened to a silvery blue. "You can't believe everything you read. Even in Rebecca's column. It was Prague, and the ladies were wearing Bohemian costumes."

"No doubt *fine vintage,*" she snapped.

He laughed. "Yeah. Costumes *and* women."

Their eyes met and her body tingled back to life. *No way. I will never ever again be sucked in by the Clayworth charm. He doesn't mean it. It's all show.*

I can see it in his eyes.

Please turn this page for praise for *Talk of the Town*...

PRAISE FOR *TALK OF THE TOWN*

"4 Stars! A funny, energetic, and charming story that's sure to entertain many readers... The depth and reality of Bodine's characters make the story come alive, and readers will finish the novel with a happy feeling inside."

—*Romantic Times BOOKreviews Magazine*
on *Talk of the Town*

"Fun, fresh, and entertaining, Bodine's work sparkles for those who like a little dish and a little romance."

—*Parkersburg News and Sentinel* (NC)

"I love this book! Fizzy, frothy fun expertly blended with sexy romance, powerful friendships, much warmth, and lots of laughter. Don't miss this witty and wonderful page-turner."

—BARBARA BRETTON, *New York Times*
bestselling author of *Casting Spells*

"Charming and a fun escape." **—JandysBooks.com**

"What a hoot! Laugh-out-loud rollicking romance... Juicy gossip, fashion advice, delish recipes, and sexy romps; *Talk of the Town* is destined to be the talk of romance readers everywhere!" **—SingleTitles.com**

"I thoroughly enjoyed *Talk of the Town*."

—ArmchairInterviews.com

ALSO BY SHERRILL BODINE

Talk of the Town

A BLACK TIE AFFAIR

SHERRILL BODINE

FOREVER

NEW YORK BOSTON

Book design by Giorgetta Bell McRee
Cover design by Melody Cassen

Forever
Hachette Book Group
237 Park Avenue
New York, NY 10017
Visit our website at www.HachetteBookGroup.com.

Forever is an imprint of Grand Central Publishing. The Forever name and logo is a trademark of Hachette Book Group, Inc.

Printed in the United States of America

First Printing: January 2010

10 9 8 7 6 5 4 3 2 1

This book was made possible by the generosity of new friend Timothy Long, curator of costumes at the Chicago History Museum and friend extraordinaire Laurie Davis, owner of LuLu's at the Belle Kay. Thank you both for introducing me into the fabulous world of vintage haute couture.

ACKNOWLEDGMENTS

CHICAGO IS FULL OF FASCINATING PLACES! Like the secret fallout shelter, now a treasure trove of historical artifacts, which I've disguised so no one can ever follow my directions.

CHICAGO IS FULL OF FASCINATING STORIES! Yes, Tim Long truly was poisoned by a black Dior evening gown, which was the inspiration for this book.

CHICAGO IS FULL OF FASCINATING CHARACTERS—many of whom I'm fortunate to call friend and who helped to bring this book to life...

Meghan Smith, who has the very best job as collection manager for costumes and textiles at the Chicago History Museum.

Dr. Alexander Stemer, supreme diagnostician and always the hero in my book.

Dr. Marc Karlan, Jack Rickard, and Tom Adams, international yachtsmen and companions on many an adventure on Lake Michigan.

Klaren Alexander, pilot, entrepreneur, and the only man I would allow to fly my private jet if I had one like his.

And

Always, I must thank Michele, Amy, Samantha, and all at Grand Central Publishing for allowing me to reveal the heart beneath Chicago's glitter.

Chicago Journal & Courier

Sunday Talk of the Town

by Rebecca Covington-Sumner

Many of us are saddened—yours truly included—by the abrupt "early retirement" of Alistair Smith, former treasurer of Chicago's iconic, exclusive department store John Clayworth and Company. Tongues are wagging about why Mr. Smith was so quickly tossed his gold watch, not to mention why he departed for Palm Beach posthaste...and methinks all the Clayworth men doth protest too much!

My heart goes out to Mr. Smith's beautiful daughters, Athena, Venus, and Diana. These lovely young women are so often compared to the internationally famous Cushing, Bouvier, and Miller sisters, all of whom made brilliant social and royal marriages.

Our Smith sisters endeared themselves to me a few years ago when they declared they were content to wait until they found their soul mates, be they princes or paupers. I can attest to the wisdom of their choices, being blissfully, madly, happy with my own Prince Charming.

Darling Athena, Venus, and Diana, hold your heads high! I'm rooting for you. And so should all of you, by attending the grand opening of Pandora's Box, their vintage couture bazaar, in honor of their late mother, Ann. And, best of all, twenty percent of all profits from Pandora's Box will go to the Ann Smith Scholarship Fund for Young Chicago Fashion Students.

As head buyer for Clayworth's, Ann had a fabulous sense of style that made the Fashions of the Hour Shop a legend within the store.

Now Pandora's Box promises to open up the secrets of Chicago's finest closets to all of us. Be there!

A BLACK TIE AFFAIR

Athena's Story

"When you enter a woman's closet, you get a glimpse into her life: who she is, who she has been, and who she has hoped to be."

CHAPTER 1

This was *the day.* The day for which Athena Smith had begged, borrowed, or stolen every favor and debt ever owed her. And now she was so late she might miss it.

On purpose?

The thought stopped Athena cold as she eyed the distance to the elegant doors of the Fashion Institute of Chicago.

No! Nothing will stop me, not even the Clayworths!

Realizing she had no other choice, she hiked up her pencil skirt and ran the last three city blocks in her favorite but impractical heels and burst through the doors.

Her tinted glasses tipped off the end of her nose, and she pushed them back into place, not to see, but to hide her real feelings when stressed. No one needed to know she wasn't like Athena, goddess of wisdom, although she always tried to be. In reality she was more like Athena, goddess of too many mistakes.

Her chest ached from the final one-block sprint as

she gazed up at Leonard, the museum's oldest security guard.

"Please tell me I'm not too late," she gasped.

He grinned yet somehow still looked solemn, as befitted his duties.

"Nope, Miss Smith. The Town Car Clayworth's Department Store sent for you and your intern is running late. They called to say they'd be here in ten minutes."

"Thanks, Leonard. You've made my day." She sighed, waved, and headed to the staircase.

The treasure trove of Bertha Palmer gowns the Clayworths had locked away in their Secret Closet danced before her eyes. It was the Holy Grail, the Golden Fleece of Chicago historic costumes.

She *shouldn't* be diving headfirst into their Secret Closet, because if she saw any of them up close and personal she'd just as likely tell them to go to hell as say, "Thank you very much for your support of the museum." But despite the wretched Clayworth men, she *would* get her hands on those dresses for the exhibit and scholarship benefit.

After all, it's my duty as curator of costumes. My duty to help fund Makayla's scholarship fund. My duty to set a good example for her. Thank God she'll be with me to remind me to behave.

Of course today was so much more important for Makayla. An opportunity like this was very rare indeed for an intern. It was one of the reasons Athena had fought so hard to make it happen.

Blissful, despite the Clayworths, that this day had finally arrived, Athena swept into the Costume Collection office.

She loved this room with its heavy carved crown moldings. Sometimes, when she stared upward, trying to brainstorm new ideas for the museum, the wood carvings looked like faces to her.

But today the rich ruby Oriental rugs and antique furniture in front of the stone fireplace didn't give off their usual cozy, old-world vibe.

Something's wrong.

Athena eyed the cup of green tea cooling on Makayla's desk. She should be here, fussing around the office like the perfect intern she'd become.

Worried, Athena headed out to find her.

She stopped when she heard the powder room door across the hall open, then close, followed by sturdy, slow, oddly heavy footsteps coming toward the office.

Makayla Elliott hopped into the room, her right foot and ankle swaddled in a thick Ace bandage.

"My God, what happened to you?" Athena rushed to help her ease down on the red velvet sofa.

"I was working last night at my part-time job at Maggiano's and I dropped a bowl of spaghetti on my foot."

Kneeling, examining Makayla's swollen toes, painted a vivid purple, Athena ached with worry. "Those bowls are big enough to feed a family of ten. Is anything broken?"

"No," Makayla shook her head so hard her black ponytail flicked her cheek. "No problem, Athena. I'm awesome, ready to go when you are."

As Makayla struggled to the edge of the sofa to stand up, Athena saw pain in her kohl-lined eyes.

In that split second, Athena swore the carved crown moldings looked like the laughing faces of those three nasty Greek Fates, Clotho, Lachesis, and Atropos, gazing back at her, secure in their absolute power of deciding everyone's destiny. Lately they'd been doing their worst with her. Well, she wouldn't let them mess with Makayla. Being orphaned, living in a group home, and working two jobs and an internship was enough already.

Laugh away, Fates. No way will I let my dear, sweet, brave Makayla traipse through the Clayworths' closet if she's in pain.

"I'm sorry. I know you're going to be disappointed, but I can't let you go today when you're in so much pain. You might do real damage to your foot. I'll do provenance on the Bertha Palmer dresses alone," Athena informed her in her best boss voice.

"No way!" Makayla wobbled to her feet, hanging on to the sofa's fat padded arm for balance. "No way...I mean..." she stammered, widening her brown eyes like she always did when worried. "I mean, I gotta go. It's an awesome opportunity for me. And what if you, like, run into any Clayworths so soon after your dad's...retirement? And I'm not there to...help you?"

Oh, no, does everyone know I want to tell them to go to hell for dear old Dad?

Disappointment for Makayla burned in her chest, but Athena plastered on her best PR smile. "Please don't worry about me. *We* at the museum *love* the Clayworths for everything they do for us. Plus, we need to convince them by hook or crook to donate the Bertha Palmer dresses to the exhibit and benefit so we can raise more money for your scholarship. *That* is more important than my feelings."

"Excuse me," Leonard called from the open door. "The Clayworth Town Car is here, Miss Smith."

Once again adjusting her glasses, Athena turned and smiled, ready for the glamour and romance of the Secret Closet, even if she must go alone.

"Thanks, Leonard. Please tell the driver I'll be right down."

She swept up the white lab coat, blue rubber gloves, and tape recorder from her desk.

"Wait, Athena." Makayla hobbled toward her, little wisps of fine dark hair clinging to her damp cheeks and her pale lips parted in a grimace of pain. "The Costume Collection manager is on maternity leave for another six weeks. You're already doing two jobs. You've got a meeting with Miss Keene tomorrow, and she's always breathing down your neck. Pandora's Box is opening on Saturday. You've got too much to do. I've gotta help you no matter what."

Gently but firmly, Athena urged Makayla back down on the sofa. "I'll handle the deputy director. Pandora's Box is ready to fling open its doors. You can help me by taking care of yourself. Put your foot up and stop making me feel guilty for depriving you of the joy of examining those beautiful gowns we've been plotting for months to get our hands on." She squeezed Makayla's warm fingers. "I'm so sorry. I know you're terribly disappointed not to go."

"It's a bummer. Everyone I know wants to see the awesome stuff the Clayworths are hiding out there. It's like an urban legend. But I don't feel so great." Makayla's lips quivered into a smile.

"I know." Looking into Makayla's pale face, so young, so earnest, Athena knew this wasn't another mistake.

"Tomorrow I *promise* to tell you *everything* about the treasures buried out there."

Sighing, Makayla lifted her foot up onto the sofa. "You're awesome, and so are your sisters and your dad. That Rebecca Covington-Sumner is right on in her column about your dad. I think the Clayworths gave him a bum deal after all the years he worked for them."

Athena blinked and curled her mouth into her "oldest-sister smile." The one she'd perfected to protect those younger and more vulnerable from learning about an unhappy possibility sooner than necessary.

Or Dad made a horrible mistake. Or he's covering something up. Otherwise surely he would have stood and fought like he taught me to do instead of running away.

Like she was fighting now to fix everything she and her dad had messed up.

Which was why, without so much as a blush, a tremble in her voice, or more than a tiny shred of guilt, Athena told the second-biggest lie of her life. "I agree with Rebecca, too."

Athena spied Bridget O'Flynn waiting next to the black Lincoln Town Car and swayed to a stop, nearly toppling off her heels.

Why in the world would the den mother to the Clayworth men and head of security for John Clayworth and Company be driving me out to the Secret Closet?

"I cleared my schedule so I could get the chance to see you," Bridget called, as if she'd read Athena's thoughts.

Before the debacle with her dad, Athena would have loved spending time with her, but right this second she wanted to run and hide like she'd been doing for weeks.

Bridget smiled at her, and Athena couldn't resist. She'd always adored her, so she smiled right back.

Walking slowly toward the car, Athena glanced around, half expecting the Clayworth brothers, who were widely known to be off overseeing their far-flung empire, to have suddenly returned to cause more problems. The way this day was going, Bridget's nephew, Connor, the stuffy lawyer with the body of a Greek god, would probably pop up in the back seat. Or, God forbid, Drew might climb out of the trunk to torment her.

She tried to think back to the days when she'd been *friends* with all the Clayworth men. Well, she'd been more than friends with Drew, but that was ancient history.

Now good manners and real affection made Athena slide into the passenger seat next to Bridget instead of hiding in the back to lick her wounds like she'd planned.

"What's wrong, Athena? Why are you still wearin' those dark glasses?" Bridget's voice held the familiar note of gruff, kind concern that made her so lovable.

"Just a bit of eye strain." Athena glanced over and got caught in Bridget's sharp green stare.

"You've been wearin' those shades since your dad left town. Have you seen a doctor?"

Athena adjusted the offending glasses, painfully aware that Bridget never minced words.

"It's nothing to worry about. I keep straining my eyes at work."

"Humph!" Bridget snorted through her aquiline nose. "Seems to me you've had nothin' but a ton of strain lately. Sure you want to visit the closet yourself today?"

"Absolutely!" Athena said with real feeling. Her fate might be sealed, but she *would* defeat it. If she saw any of the Clayworth men, she'd simply shove them out of her way and get to those clothes. "*Everyone* wants a peek into that closet. Mom once told me that in the old days they covered the eyes of all who went out there because of the treasures locked away in its depths." She slid Bridget a hopeful look. "Are you going to put a blindfold on me? Any Clayworth skeletons for me to find out there?"

Bridget chuckled. "No skeletons and no blindfolds. I trust you." She gunned the high-horsepower engine. "All right, then. Rest your eyes a while. We'll be there in about an hour. Dependin' on traffic."

Athena turned her head toward the window, but she couldn't close her eyes. Now that she was on her way to the family's top-secret fallout shelter, built beneath a farmer's field during the Cold War, which currently housed many of their treasures, including Bertha's priceless gowns, excitement made her feel warm all over, like it had her entire life. Like she'd felt when word came that the Clayworth family had agreed to the museum's request to examine the dresses for possible inclusion in the exhibit.

Why had they agreed? Guilt? For old times' sake?

Their tangled friendships were such old, old news. Yet since her dad's firing, the Clayworths and everything they'd meant to her filled her mind nearly every waking moment. She shoved them away *again,* determined to focus on her goal of doing provenance on the department store's impressive, never-before-seen collection of vintage couture clothing.

Warm and eager, she watched the city fade away into flat prairie. Travel on I90 appeared lighter than normal. Thirty minutes later, Bridget exited onto a two-lane highway. She seemed to know the road by heart, anticipating the bad patches and the sharp twists. Prairie gave way to slightly rolling cornfields. Bridget slowed and turned onto a one-lane black-tar road. She sped up, a clear, smooth stretch of road before them. All at once the tar turned to gravel and Bridget made a sharp right onto a bumpy dirt track leading into a soybean field.

She braked to a halt, and Athena, getting more eager by the second, sat up straighter. They were plop in the middle of Midwest farmland, surrounded by low soybean sprouts and rustling stalks of short young corn.

Athena pressed her nose to the window. "There's nothing here."

Bridget laughed. "They built it so it couldn't be seen from the air. Look again."

When she'd been a child whiling away the long, hot summer afternoons, lying on the grass in their back yard in Lincoln Park, Athena's family would play the cloud game. She squinted her eyes looking for the secret. Once she'd been the best at spotting everything from her cat, Drusilla, to the Field Museum in the clouds, and once, absolutely, she still swore to this day, she saw Abraham Lincoln in his top hat.

In this case, at first she thought she must be simply gazing at good black Illinois dirt, but no.

I've found it!

A steel door big enough to back a semi trailer into. The rolling field of soybeans directly in front of her had to be the roof.

"I see it!" Athena quickly stepped out and followed Bridget to the enormous black wall. She paused to read the sign engraved into the steel: "When the alarm sounds, a blast has occurred. You have three minutes to get inside."

"Gives you the willies, doesn't it?" Bridget shuddered. "Wait until you see the rest." She punched a code into the panel on a smaller door, barely visible, and led Athena into silent blackness.

Athena blinked, allowing her eyes to adjust to the dim, vast cavern looming in front of her. She pulled off her glasses to get a better look.

The cooler air sent goose bumps crawling along her arms, and she rubbed them away. "This constant underground temperature is the best storage."

Beside her, Bridget chuckled. "You don't need to whisper. Let me turn on more lights so you can see the place. It's a real time capsule."

The harsh glare of fluorescent lights made Athena blink again. Now she could see they were standing in a small entrance to the huge cave that stretched out before her. To her right loomed an oven big enough to roast an ox.

"This is the decontamination chamber." Bridget moved briskly forward. "That oven is the incinerator where we would have burned our clothes." She glanced back, her wide smile splitting her pale face. "I guess they would have been naked as the day they were born until they got to the bedroom."

Athena burst out laughing. "The Clayworth men running around naked. Now, there's a sight half the women in Chicago have dreamed about seeing."

Bridget shook her head. "Those boys are too good-lookin' for their own good. I fear half of those ladies have had their dreams come true."

And I'm one of them.

She felt herself getting warmer.

Bridget shot her a sharp, inquisitive look. "Are you all right?"

"Great! Love it. What's next?"

"The bedrooms."

Athena followed Bridget into a room lined with rows of bunk beds and one appropriately green-tiled 1950s-style bathroom. Beyond she saw a kitchen with appliances in the same color and a Formica dinette set, straight out of a vintage television sitcom.

"What kind of clothes did you find here when they decided to turn it into their Secret Closet?" Athena asked. The curator in her was already planning an exhibit of what would have been worn in a fallout shelter like this one during the Cold War.

"Don't know. Back in the day they must have planned to have somethin' to wear while they were here." She pointed to a chain-link fence holding back small boulders stretching out for six yards beyond the kitchen. "The idea was to stay down here for two years. Then tear apart this fence holdin' back rocks. Dig their way out into what was left of the world." Bridget shook her head so hard the gold clip holding up her white-streaked strawberry curls came loose. With a yank she shoved it firmly back in place. "Whole thing was crazy. But the vault was the craziest of all."

Totally entranced, Athena followed her deeper into the cavernous underground shelter. They passed row after row of the store's famous glass-window wagons and a fleet of electric broughams, all with the famous John Clayworth and Company logo brazened in gold letters on the side.

They stopped in front of the largest safe door she'd ever seen, even in pictures of the U.S. Mint.

Using both hands, Bridget turned the giant tumbler. "They built this to keep the credit records of all the store's customers." She snorted. "Like anyone would care about their bills when the world's comin' to an end." She swung the door wide open. "Now all that foolishness is behind us, they store Bertha's gowns in here."

A golden glow fell out into the gloom. Light glistened off rhinestones, silver cord, and gold beads.

The four Bertha Palmer dresses beckoned Athena into their world, the way mythology had, when her father made it come alive. Her senses dazzled by the dresses worn by one of her mother's idols, dresses that when used properly could make her dreams come true, Athena rushed past Bridget into the vault.

Struck by a blast of warm air, she gasped. "The temperature in here should be better controlled. And these dresses shouldn't be on mannequins. They should be in their own specially built archival boxes."

"Good golly, you almost sound like your old self." Bridget laughed. "That's the spirit. You and your sisters used to give those boys hell when you were youngsters. They need to be put in their place once in a while."

Part of her would like nothing better than to tell the Clayworths what she thought of them for casting her father aside so cavalierly, but she had to put the past behind her to get what she needed.

Maybe I'm wrong again.

She slowly shook her head. "Maybe it's just me. It's probably cool enough. I'm just so thrilled to be here, I'm feverish with anticipation. It's an honor for the museum to have the opportunity to establish the provenance on these dresses."

Bridget cocked her head, slanting a long glance into Athena's deliberately blank face. "Sure you're all right with all of this?"

"Sure. Can't wait to get my fingers on these dresses." She tried to beam good cheer but felt naked not being able to hide behind the glasses she'd rammed into the lab coat pocket. She turned away to slip on the coat and rubber gloves. "I'll get to work. I don't want to keep you here all day."

"I'd best leave you to it, then." Bridget sighed. "If you need me, I'll be in the kitchen doin' paperwork."

Athena nodded without looking around. She sensed Bridget wanted to say more, but Athena couldn't discuss her dad now. It still felt too raw.

Determined to push away every thought except these dresses, she stepped in front of the first mannequin. Her breath caught in a tremble of excitement before she spoke into her tiny handheld tape recorder.

"I'm here in the Clayworth family Secret Closet to establish provenance on four Bertha Palmer gowns. I am starting with a dress of black corded grenadine with green and pink stripes over green taffeta. Trimmed with loops of narrow pink satin and green grosgrain ribbons."

Unable to resist, she delicately traced the bodice with her fingertips. "The bodice is made to look like a corselette of black satin with jet passementerie interlaced with narrow pink satin ribbon outlined with one-and-one-fourth-inch double-faced satin ribbon."

She dropped to her knees to peer up into the sleeves, again reverently touching the exquisite, delicate fabric.

"The small leg-of-mutton sleeves are lined to the elbow with green taffeta."

Wanting to better view the workmanship, she stretched out on the concrete floor. The cold seeped through her lab coat, thin cashmere sweater, and cotton skirt.

Shivering, she carefully lifted the hem of the gown and peered up inside. "The skirt is gored with gathers at the back. Blind pocket of white taffeta lined with soft green fine rep silk taffeta. The construction is exquisite. There are twelve bones in the bodice. Each is sewn with stitches so tiny and fine I can barely see them."

Something kept irritating the back of her throat, and she stifled a cough. "Bertha Palmer wore this gown in the summer months, and it is reported to have been one of her favorites."

Her voice hoarse from holding back the cough, she slid out from beneath the gown to clear her throat. She brushed at her cheeks, trying to get rid of whatever tickled her skin.

The second mannequin, the one on her right, began to shimmer, giving it the sudden, odd appearance of movement.

She shook her head, trying to clear it. Instead the world spun slowly around and a rush of euphoria made her giddy. Happier than she'd felt in months. She didn't understand what was happening to her, but right now, here, she didn't care.

She giggled, doing a little dance to the gown. Her body tingled with recklessness, daring her to do something forbidden. Like the time she dared Drew to go skinny dipping with her in the pond at the far end of the Clayworth estate in Lake Forest.

She shook her head to clear her thoughts. *Away with you!* she commanded. But the memory wouldn't obey. She just kept swelling and swelling with the same excitement and fear she'd felt then, knowing if her parents found out she'd be sent to boarding school. She ripped off her gloves to stroke the heavy champagne silk satin gown with her bare fingers.

She'd seen countless pictures of this famous Worth gown when Mrs. Potter Palmer wore it at the Court of Saint James's in London, but the photos didn't do it justice. It mesmerized her. Totally irresistible.

Athena slid her fingertips down the elegant, heavy white velvet train and lifted it around her shoulders, wrapping herself in its beauty. Again and again she traced the white satin iris design, each flower done by hand, which made the dress so unique, so special. She turned the train over in her arms so the lining of silver tissue and rhinestone edging glistened back at her.

Seeing and touching this gown made her feel connected to her mom's passion for vintage haute couture fashion. She had been the epitome of beauty and had taught Athena to appreciate the grace of this lost world.

She ached to slide her body up and through the princess-style dress the way Bertha would have done. She ran the old, soft silk tulle along her neck and arms, loving the feel of it.

Drawn by the exquisite detail of the double white net ruffle around the hem, she sank down upon her knees and then lay on her back. She scooted beneath the skirt to look up at the white taffeta lining. She brushed her hot cheek against the cool fabric and sighed.

It felt so cool, so comforting she didn't want to move.

The dress fell around her like a wedding veil, beautiful yet protective. She felt content to merely lie beneath the gown, breathing in its history. She wanted to stay here forever, safe in Bertha's kinder, gentler world. She heard a string quartet playing a waltz like they would have done that afternoon in London for Bertha. Athena closed her eyes, lost in the music, lost in a world she adored. Far away from the reality of the last few months.

She floated in peace until the musicians started repeating the same stanza, over and over and over again. She opened her eyes, angry at this rude, discordant interruption of her bliss.

"Athena! Athena! Athena! Can you hear me? Athena! Athena!" Bridget called excessively. "Come out from under that skirt. You've been lyin' there for an hour!"

Athena tried to shake off Bridget's strong hands tugging at her ankle, but she couldn't. "No, I don't want to come out. I like it here," she shouted back.

"Athena, if you don't come out, I'm comin' in after you," Bridget called and gave another hard tug at Athena's foot.

Not wanting to be rude, Athena sighed and crawled out. After all, she *loved* Bridget—at this moment she *loved* everyone.

Blinking, she looked up.

It isn't Bridget!

Bertha Palmer, Chicago's proud social queen of the late 1800s and early 1900s, stood smiling down at her.

Athena screamed, scrambling to her feet. "This isn't a time capsule, it's a time warp! Bertha, you're really here!"

Joy exploded through her hot, throbbing body. She

gripped Bertha's small, cool hands. "My mother *loved* you and what you did for Chicago. She loved powerful women of the past who blazed a trail for the rest of us."

Out of the corner of her eye, she caught a blur of movement, like someone else had come. She looked around but couldn't focus her eyes. She shook her head, trying to stop the slowly spinning world. "Is someone else here, too?" She looked toward the last shimmering mannequin and blinked. Jackie Kennedy, wearing her famous blue pillbox hat and coatdress, stood watching her.

"Jackie, you're here, too!" Athena called to her. "Mom said you were just like Bertha and knew the power of dress."

The world spun faster and faster, making Bertha blur and Jackie vanish. Fearful she'd lost both of them, Athena gripped Bertha's hand tighter. "Where did Jackie go?"

"Come with me, Athena. I saw Jackie go this way, toward the front."

She laughed in relief and joy, twining her fingers through Bertha's and running with her toward the harsh fluorescent lights in the decontamination chamber.

Outside, the sky looked so penetratingly blue its brightness hurt her eyes. She squeezed her lids closed. "I can't see Jackie anymore. Which way did she go?"

"I see her, Athena. This way. Climb into the back seat of the car and we'll follow her."

Athena opened her aching eyes the tiniest bit to glance up at Bertha. For a brief instant a vivid gold encircled Bertha's curls like a halo. Athena sighed. "You look just as beautiful as I knew you were. You were Mom's absolute favorite. She called you Chicago's angel."

"That's nice. In you go, Athena."

The back seat smelled like new leather. Athena's lids felt too heavy to leave open. She closed them just as she heard the loud, powerful car motor roar to life.

"Can you still see Jackie?" Athena whispered, so tired she couldn't lift her head.

"Yes. Don't you worry. Everythin' will be fine. You rest now. I'm turnin' on some nice, soothin' music for you."

Athena floated in a strange twilight contentment more profound than she'd experienced beneath Bertha's exquisite gown. This time when the music came, it had words. "God Bless the Child."

"I love this song." The words vibrated through her head, and she began to hum the tune to herself. A burst of energy and joy exploded through her blood. Her voice sounded so pure and true and golden, she let the words pour from her throat.

Holding the last note, she lost track of her breathing. The twilight world behind her eyes swirled crazily around, blue, purple, orange, and, at last, a cool blackness. She rested again, floating contentedly in silent bliss.

CHAPTER 2

On any other perfect spring day like this in Chicago, Drew Clayworth would be sailing on Lake Michigan.

Today he kept his old Morgan 46 securely docked.

The wind called him like it always did, flowing around the mast, cool against his skin, bringing the taste of adventure and freedom. Irresistible. Drew took a deep breath, holding the flavor in his lungs, before he deliberately let it go, refusing to be lured today by sailing's siren call. Instead he patiently listened to the complaints of the three teenage boys who were struggling into their orange life jackets and not happy about it.

Washington Thomas sneered up at him. "Hey, man, thought you were teachin' us how to sail this tub."

Drew grinned, meeting the eyes of Jefferson Adams, his first mate. Jeff had given him this same line of bravado three years ago, the first kid from the Youth Center Drew taught to sail.

"Yeah, I'm teaching you to sail this tub," Drew drawled back. "First lesson is safety."

"I ain't afraid of shit." Bruce Madison laughed. "I can sure as hell swim good."

"Shut up, dog. I can't so good," Calvin Tremont, the smallest of the three, shouted to his friend.

Drew reached out and tightened Calvin's life jacket, shifting it into place before meeting the eyes of all the boys. "Your goal is to stay out of the water. When sailing, the biggest threat to your life is hypothermia. Today the water temperature in Lake Michigan is fifty degrees. That means if you went overboard for fifty minutes, you'd have a fifty percent better chance of surviving wearing a life jacket."

Everyone glanced at the seemingly benign waves lapping at the hull—except Calvin. He shot Drew a scared, wide-eyed appeal.

"Don't worry. I'll keep you safe," he muttered to him, meaning every word.

"You goin' to jump in and save me?" Washington taunted, balancing on the bow to get attention.

Drew got half the distance to Washington when Jeff grabbed the kid by the scruff of his neck and hauled him back from the edge.

"Hey, punk, I jumped in the water once, and if Mr. Clayworth hadn't hauled my ass out I'd have froze my dick off. This is serious business."

"Jokin' around, dude." Washington shrugged away. "I dig that Mr. Clayworth's the man."

"The man to keep us safe, right?" Calvin moved a step closer.

"Right, Calvin. I'll teach you all to save yourselves by

being smart and prepared. Let's get your safety equipment on. Jeff, give me a hand here."

Fifteen years of regret burned in Drew's gut while he worked on the straps of Bruce's life jacket. Fifteen years of guilt and regret that he couldn't keep his parents safe. He needed to put it all to rest. Find closure with their decisions and his.

I will. Soon.

Lost in his plans, he didn't hear the phone buzzing in his windbreaker until Jeff nodded toward his pocket.

Drew shook his head, ignoring it. He needed to get the kids organized.

The damn phone kept buzzing. He yanked it out. "Christ, Connor, I'll be back at Clayworth's in an hour. I'm teaching the kids now," he barked out at his cousin.

"Drew, I'm at Northwestern Hospital with Aunt Bridget."

Fear cut through him like a steel blade, but he didn't flinch, didn't give anything away.

"What's wrong with Bridget?" he asked, maintaining the outward calm he'd had to learn at nineteen.

"It's not Aunt Bridget."

He heard the relief in Connor's voice and felt the same rush of emotion. Bridget was his family, too.

"Something happened out at the Secret Closet. Aunt Bridget brought Athena Smith to the ER."

Athena's tear-streaked face from a lifetime ago flashed in front of Drew's eyes.

A different emotion drove him across the deck. He turned his back, not wanting anyone to read his face. "What happened to Athena?"

"She's disoriented and hallucinating. The resident on duty is examining her, but they can't find—"

"Call Lewis Stemmer. Now!" Drew interrupted. "He's the best diagnostician in the country. If he can't find out what's wrong, no one can. I'll be there in half an hour."

He swung back to find Jeff watching him.

"Got a problem, Mr. Clayworth?"

"Yeah, I need to go, but the van from the center for the kids won't be here for twenty minutes."

Jeff squared his shoulders. "I can handle it. Don't worry. I won't let you down."

Drew hesitated, wanting to stay to keep everyone safe, needing to go for his family, hoping to trust the determined expression on Jeff's face.

Need and hope won out.

He turned back to the waiting boys. "Guys, Jeff will show you the safety features of this Morgan 46. I'll see you next week."

Calvin's eyes darted between Jeff and Drew. "You say so?"

"Yeah, I say it's good." He looked at Jeff, already talking to Washington and Bruce, and knew it was true.

Drew sprinted down the gangplank and along the dock. He hunched his shoulders against the stiff, cold wind chopping at the lake. A new weather front had come in. If he believed in omens, this would be one.

Athena Smith coming back into his life now meant trouble.

"I've told you both ten times, I've never felt better in my life. I'm sick with worry about Athena. I got her here. Now we've got to help her."

Drew heard Bridget's voice before he saw her, Connor, and Lewis Stemmer in a corner of the ER waiting room.

She looked up and sighed. "Thank the good Lord you've come, Drew. We've got to help Athena."

"We will." He bent and kissed her cheek before he shook Lewis's hand. "Thanks for coming. Have you seen Athena?"

Cool, collected, always self-confident, Lewis nodded, and Drew felt the odd catch in his chest ease up.

Whatever's wrong can be fixed.

"I've examined her. I'm waiting for the toxicity and blood work. Her vitals are good. She's conscious now. She is still experiencing intermittent disorientation and hallucinations." Lewis's calm voice held all their attention.

"Whatever happened to Athena out at the closet, we'll get the blame. Damn it, we shouldn't have agreed to this in the first place. Now add up this mess, the rumors about the store and Alistair, plus how the Smith sisters feel about us, and we've got a lawsuit on our hands." Connor narrowed his eyes, much like his Aunt Bridget's.

Hers shot green fire at him. "Spoken like a true lawyer, and you may be right. But you need to lighten up and stop always thinkin' the worst. Wish you weren't such a tight-butt like your mom."

Connor's mouth fell open, Lewis studied Bridget over the top of his wire-rimmed glasses, and Drew looked down to hide his smile. He knew truer words were never spoken about Connor. But coming from Bridget, they were a shocker.

What the hell is going on?

She clasped her hands over her mouth. "Don't know why I said that. Love you to death, Connor, just the way you are. Always have. Always will."

Bridget cast her slightly unfocused gaze in Drew's direction. "You've been the smartest one of the boys since kindergarten. I suppose you think it's your job to go charm Athena like you do everyone else on the planet. I know it's your job to fix things for Clayworth's, but you know what? You need to fix things for yourself. It's more than time. Right now, though, you and I need to go see about Athena. Is it hot in here?" Bridget asked in her next breath and pulled the carefully folded handkerchief out of Connor's blazer pocket to fan herself.

Lewis slid down next to her. "Bridget, I think you should stay here and rest while Drew visits with Athena. She's been asking to see him."

In a day full of shocks, *this* one stopped him.

If Athena is asking for me, she really is hallucinating.

Connor hovered beside Bridget, who had shut her eyes. "What are you waiting for, Drew? Keep communication open so we know what we're facing. But remember, we can't discuss the situation with her father until we have more answers."

He nodded. Christ, he didn't know what the hell had happened to everyone out at the Secret Closet, but his job would always be to keep Clayworth's safe, so he needed to find out. "Where is she?"

"I had her moved to room one. Her sisters are with her," Lewis said.

Triple trouble.

"I'll be back."

Drew moved through the ER, dodging nurses and

interns taking care of patients in rooms three, four, and five. A few guys stood at the main desk, staring at Venus and Diana Smith hovering outside the glass partition to room one.

He didn't blame them. People always used the word *beautiful* to describe the Smith sisters. A man could drown in their large and luminous aquamarine eyes. Once, Athena's eyes had taken his breath away. Maybe the two interns drooling over her sisters from across the room were feeling the same slow burn in their guts.

But Drew knew what they didn't. A prudent man needed to tread carefully when confronted by the combined forces of the Smith sisters.

When they saw him coming, Venus threw herself in front of the door and Diana, a head shorter, stepped in front of her.

"We should have known your family would send for reinforcements. Go away," Venus muttered, tossing ropes of apricot hair over her shoulder.

Yeah, I remember. Middle child.

Diana, hands on hips, stared up at him. "I'm sure Dr. Stemmer told you Athena's calling for you. Obviously, she was hallucinating. Earlier she thought we were both our mother. She seems fine now. I don't think—"

"Diana," Drew said, smiling to soften his interruption. "Lewis Stemmer is the best doctor in the state. If he thinks I should see Athena, I should."

Through the half-closed door, he heard Athena's voice, faint and muttering.

Diana glanced up at her sister. "I think she's calling his name again. Maybe we should let him in if Dr. Stemmer thinks it's a good idea."

"Five minutes. Not a second more," Venus snapped, stepping out of the way.

He walked past them into the small cubicle and closed the door.

The light over the hospital bed fell on Athena, making her skin look like polished marble and her hair shine like gold. She'd always been the most beautiful of the sisters. Admitting it jarred the other memories of her that he'd buried.

Athena slowly opened her eyes, and he sucked in a deep breath.

"Drew, you didn't go!" she gasped, then sat straight up in bed and held out her arms to him.

Christ, he didn't know what to do. Was she faking? Playing some sort of game with him? He knew she couldn't be trusted.

She grabbed his hand, and he let her tug him down beside her. He'd taught himself to hide his emotions, and he hoped he had erased the surprise from his face.

Slowly, he forced a smile. "Athena—"

"Shh." She cupped his face in her hands and kissed his mouth. Her lips were velvety, warm, full.

Shock held him next to her. Déjà vu. Like life rewound so he could change it this time.

Anger at her, at himself, jarred him away. He hated the way his pulse pounded.

He needed to take control of the situation. "Athena, I'm here—"

She placed her fingertips over his lips. "Please, let me talk first. Oh, Drew, I've missed you so." She pressed against him, and all Drew's blood rushed to his head, like a broken dam, filling his mind with old memories of her. He knew she'd always been a good actress. Lewis had said *intermittent* hallucinations. Diana had said she seemed fine now.

If Athena's playing, I'm willing to go along to get at the truth.

He let her trace his jaw line with her lips, holding his feelings in an iron grip.

"You taste the same." Once again she cupped his face and stared into his eyes. He didn't flinch nor drown in their depths. "I'm so happy you didn't go. I'm so happy you understand why I did it."

Sighing, she collapsed against his chest. "Oh, Drew, I've been so confused about you and my dad and everything. Will you help me figure it all out?" She tilted her cheek against his shoulder and gazed up at him, her eyes fathomless aquamarine pools. "Promise you'll help me. Like you've always done."

His pulse did another odd skip. Probably anger at the young fool he'd once been.

He stared down into her beautiful face, remembering the last time she'd made him a promise.

What's one more lie between us?

"Yeah, I promise to help you. But first you need to close your eyes and try to sleep."

With the innate charm that had carried the Smith sisters into the hearts and minds of more than their fair share of men, Athena gave him a dazzling smile and slowly lowered her eyelids.

He eased her back onto the pillows and stood up. He backed out of the room, trying to figure out what the hell was going on and what he could do to minimize the damage.

Venus and Diana hovered outside in the hall. "We need to talk to Lewis Stemmer. Come with me," he commanded, once again in control.

In the ER waiting room, Connor still hovered over Bridget. To Drew, her eyes looked too bright. Like Athena's had.

Lewis beckoned them to the quiet corner. "All right. Here's what I've got." Lewis threw a long glance at the circle gathered around him. "My diagnosis is always based fifteen percent on tests, five percent on my physical exam, and eighty percent on questioning the patient. At the moment I can't get answers from Athena, so I need to get them from all of you."

Lewis leaned closer to Bridget. "Tell me about Athena's behavior in the car on the way to the closet."

"A little quiet. Everythin' seemed fine until we got to the vault."

"What happened then, Bridget? Did you see anything? Smell anything?"

"It's chilly down there. Which Athena said was good for storage. She was actin' just fine until I found her lyin' on the floor with her head up the skirt of a beautiful champagne-colored gown. The one with the train." Bridget gazed around at all of them. "When I made her come out from under it, she looked stoned. And started talkin' like I was Bertha Palmer herself and Jackie Kennedy was roamin' through the closet."

Drew glanced at her sisters. "Does Athena do recreational drugs?"

"Athena hardly takes aspirin," Venus snapped.

Drew met Lewis's eyes before he turned back to Bridget. "What happened in the car before she passed out?"

A grimace of pain flashed across Bridget's face. "I put in a CD, thinkin' the music might relax her. She started singin' at the top of her lungs."

Drew didn't miss the look passing between the sisters or the way Venus bit her lip.

Yeah, I remember, too.

Diana smiled sweetly at Bridget. "I'm sorry."

"You'll never find a more beautiful young woman, inside or out, than your sister. But I've never heard worse caterwaulin' in my life. Worried sick about her, though. What's the matter with all of you?" Bridget glared at Lewis. "Drew says you're the best, so you must be. Tell us what's wrong so we can fix it."

Unflappable, Lewis nodded. "I believe Athena has been exposed to a toxic substance that caused a rapid adverse neurological reaction. It could conceivably be four other illnesses, so I'm prescribing antibiotic and saline drips to cover a broad spectrum. I'm admitting her and moving her to the third floor as soon as I can find a room. I expect the effects of the toxic substance to have worn off by morning." Lewis studied Bridget's flushed face. "I've been observing you, and I believe you were exposed to the same toxin but to a much lesser degree."

"I feel great." Bridget flung up her head and laughed. "In fact, if I can't do any more to help Athena, I'm headin' home to snuggle with Connor's uncle Tony."

"Way to go, Aunt Bridget," Venus muttered, heading back to room one with her sister.

Connor shot her his narrow lawyer look before he followed Bridget, who marched toward the exit.

Drew couldn't help the worry eating at him, even

though he knew Connor would take care of her. "Do you want us to talk Bridget back in here?" he asked Lewis.

"No need. I took Bridget's vitals while you were seeing Athena. I'm positive that Bridget will experience nothing more than a pleasant euphoria or I wouldn't have let her leave."

"Good. Then what else should we be doing?"

"We need to get all four of those Bertha Palmer dresses out of the Secret Closet and in my lab by ten o'clock tomorrow morning."

"Done."

Drew's instincts told him he would get to the bottom of whatever had affected Athena, and he would make sure no one else became infected.

Those same instincts warned him that doing so might involve keeping his promise to Athena, after all.

CHAPTER 3

Athena forced her eyes open, and her black world with shots of orange around the edges disappeared. Now she was in a swirling white mist. She blinked and saw her sisters' disembodied heads, wearing shockingly solemn expressions, floating toward her.

This isn't right.

She blinked again and kept blinking until the mist cleared so she saw Venus and Diana's heads were definitely attached to their bodies. *Her* body ached all over, especially where an IV needle stuck out of her right arm.

"Why am I in the hospital? Is Bridget all right? Did we have a car wreck?" Her mouth felt dry and her voice sounded thin.

Venus broke into a wide smile. "Bridget is fine. And so are you."

Snatches of scenes drifted through her aching head. Clayworth Secret Closet. Bridget. Bertha's dresses.

Woozy, like she'd had too much champagne, but without the memory of a good time, she inched herself higher on the bed pillows. "The last thing I remember is lying beneath the Bertha Palmer gown she wore to her presentation at the Court of Saint James's. What happened to me?"

"While you were examining the gown, you started hallucinating about Bertha Palmer."

Athena's head and body throbbed all over with a dull, constant ache, sicker than she'd ever felt, but she knew she couldn't be at death's door or even close to it, or Diana wouldn't sound so calm. She looked closely at her sisters.

"You both look like you've slept in your clothes. Did you two stay with me all night?"

"Naturally. You were so out of it you thought you were actually visited by Bertha's ghost." Venus shivered with her usual drama. "Wish I'd been there. I'd love to ask the old girl about her jewelry."

"I would have loved to meet Jackie O. She had such impeccable taste," Diana sighed.

"I thought I saw both of them?" Athena gasped.

Venus nodded. "That's why Bridget rushed you to the ER. And before you passed out in the back seat, you were singing at the top of your lungs."

Singing. The word caught in Athena's splitting headache. "Oh, my God. Poor Bridget." She tried to gather her scattered senses to understand why she'd suddenly lost her mind. "What do the doctors think is wrong with me?"

"Drew Clayworth sent Lewis Stemmer to examine you. He's the very best infectious-disease doctor and toxicology specialist in Chicago."

Venus tossed her hair over her shoulder. "Then Drew insisted on seeing you for himself."

Drew Clayworth.

The instant she heard his name, her sisters' voices slowly faded away. Images took living, breathing form around her.

I'm still hallucinating!

A 3-D home video played around her hospital bed.

She *felt* the frigid December air, *saw* the light snow falling, perfect for Christmas Eve, glistening off Drew's hair and skin. *Heard* her heels clicking on the dark flagstone terrace of the Clayworth mansion in Lake Forest. Drew looked up and saw her. His blue eyes pools of grief.

"I'm alone and it's my fault. The race was my idea, and my parents died because of it. Because of me," he whispered.

Her young heart splintered, and she wanted to give each and every piece to him. She knelt in front of him and cupped his face. "No, no, it's not your fault. You're not alone. I love you. I've always loved you, and nothing will ever ever make me stop loving you."

He stared at her so long and hard she'd thought she'd die of longing.

"I believe you love me," he whispered and crushed her to him the way she'd always dreamed.

Athena blinked, willing the images to go away before she saw the ending yet again. She'd replayed it in her head *too* many times.

"I don't remember seeing Drew very much after his parents were killed in that terrible sailing accident when he was nineteen," Diana said quietly. "It almost seemed like he avoided us after he moved in with the Henry Clayworth clan."

Athena knew he'd been avoiding *her.*

She forced herself to focus on her sisters, who were glaring at each other like they did whenever Diana said anything that remotely cast the Clayworth posse in a good light. Venus always disagreed with her, and soon their voices would reach a fever pitch of sisterly bickering.

"Please don't argue. My head hurts enough already. I don't remember seeing a doctor or Drew. Was I still unconscious when they were here?"

"Far from it. You were calling for Drew."

"No fair teasing, Venus. I'm too weak to fight back." Athena shut her eyes, wishing this whole thing was one long hallucination. She opened them again and looked up at her more serious sister. "She's teasing, right?"

Diana shook her head. "I don't know why, but you kept calling for him, so we let him in."

The thought made her so weak she sank deeper into the pillows. "What did I say to him?" she whispered, dread nearly choking her.

"We couldn't hear anything through the closed door," Venus admitted with a frown.

"Did anyone bother to tell you why I've lost my mind?"

Diana patted her arm. "Do you want us to locate Dr. Stemmer and find out what's going on?"

"Please," she whispered, needing to get out of here before she made an even bigger fool of herself.

Her headstrong sisters quickly and silently left the room, but at the door Venus turned to mouth, "We'll be right back," and Diana gave her a thumbs-up.

Comforted by the knowledge that support would be only a shout away, Athena closed her eyes.

"How are you feeling, Athena? Dr. Stemmer will be here in a few minutes."

Shock opened her eyes, and for the first time in fifteen years Athena looked up straight into Drew Clayworth's eyes.

Sure, she'd glimpsed him across crowded ballrooms at black tie affairs, large cocktail parties, any number of places, but she'd never purposely *looked* at him.

Yes, he really did look exactly like the vintage poster of Paul Newman in Hollywood's version of *Cat on a Hot Tin Roof* she'd once hung on her bedroom wall because it reminded her of Drew. Every feature from brow to lips seemingly chiseled in stone. His close-cropped fair hair made his eyes appear even more startlingly cornflower blue, piercing and crinkled at the corners with a smile.

A far cry from the deadly serious, hurt glare he'd flung her the last time they'd been together.

A burst of warmth exploded inside her, and all at once the hospital sheet felt heavy against her skin. She pushed it down the tiniest bit with her free hand.

In two strides Drew reached her bedside. "How are you feeling?"

The world tilted slightly to the right, and she bit her lip to stop the crazy thoughts racing through her mind.

I know most women in Chicago would love having you hover over their beds. But I'm immune to you. Have been for years since you told me exactly what you think of me. And I'm here to tell you I feel the same way about you after what your family did to my dad. I don't trust you any further than I could throw you.

"Athena, what's wrong?" Drew asked sharply and leaned closer to her.

"I'm sorry I'm late." A tall, handsome man she'd never seen before came striding through the door. "Hello, Drew. Athena, how are you feeling this morning?"

With a thud that rattled her insides, the world settled back on its axis and sanity returned. "Better. Thank you," she gasped, the room coming into crystal-clear focus.

A ghost of a smile curled Drew's long, full mouth. It vanished so quickly she might have imagined it, considering she'd been seeing other ghosts lately.

To hide her confusion, she swept her dark glasses up off the bedside table and slipped them on.

"You must be Dr. Stemmer come to tell me why I've lost my mind."

"You haven't lost your mind, Athena."

Dr. Stemmer spoke with such utter assurance she actually felt the tiniest bit less panicked at wanting to brazenly tell Drew what she really thought of him.

"After studying your blood test results, I believe you were exposed to toxic fumes or particles that caused a rapid and adverse neurological reaction. The effects can mirror those of being exposed to Sodium Pentothal, the so-called truth serum."

"Truth serum." The thought of what she might have done made her feel sick again. She purposely concentrated on Dr. Stemmer and tried to ignore Drew's looming presence.

"Is Bridget all right? Is she hallucinating, too? She was in that vault, too, breathing the same toxic air."

"I checked on her this morning. Bridget is fine. She didn't have any direct close contact with the four Bertha

Palmer gowns the way you did, so she wasn't as severely affected."

Thank God she had on her dark glasses so neither Drew nor the doctor could see her shock. "What do you mean? What do the gowns have to do with it?"

"Bridget told us she found you underneath the skirt of a dress you'd been examining for an hour. I suspect the gown itself is toxic." Dr. Stemmer glanced down at his pager. "I'm sorry. I need to go. I'll have the nurse take you off the IV drips. Rest now. I'll be back to see you later."

Some memory tried to fight its way out of her aching head, but she couldn't quite grab it. She gave up to make sense of what Dr. Stemmer had just told her.

"I can't believe Bertha's gown had anything to do with this," she said to Drew, who still hovered by her bed.

"I can," Drew answered with the usual Clayworth confidence. "Lewis Stemmer is the best. He knows what he's talking about."

No doubt her face looked as hot as she felt consumed with another odd spurt of truthfulness. "Drew, I beg Dr. Stemmer's pardon, but not yours. Neither one of you knows as much about Bertha's gowns as I do. I'm an expert on vintage clothing and have had my head up dozens more skirts than either one of you."

Now she couldn't mistake his smile. It curled his beautiful mouth deep at the corners. "In that department I can't speak for Dr. Stemmer. Only myself."

The Clayworth confidence, *and* the Clayworth reputation with women, set her on fire. She thrust up her chin. "*Probably* I've had my head up more skirts than you. Vintage ones for sure!"

"That's debatable," he muttered, lowering his lids for an instant over those cornflower eyes.

I'm going to do it again.

She tried not to open her mouth. She ran her free hand around the neck of the hospital gown to let in some air to cool her hot, heaving bosom. Anything to stop herself.

"Of course, how could I possibly have forgotten," she drawled, helpless not to. "I remember the item Rebecca ran about you and your cousins closing down a restaurant in Paris while cavorting with a troupe of topless can-can dancers."

His lips twitched, and his eyes lightened to a silvery blue. "You can't believe everything you read. Even in Rebecca's column. It was Prague, and the ladies were wearing Bohemian costumes."

"No doubt *fine vintage,*" she snapped.

He laughed. "Yeah. Costumes *and* women."

Their eyes met, and her body tingled back to life.

No way. I will never ever again be sucked in by the Clayworth charm. He doesn't mean it. It's all show. I can see it in his eyes.

She thrust her chin so high, her neck ached. "Your global escapades with your cousins don't make you an expert on vintage couture. *I am one.* And I've never been overcome before, or found any garment remotely toxic. Obviously, I was *overcome* by some toxic matter you Clayworths are hoarding in your store's top-secret closet!"

"I'll be able to confirm Dr. Stemmer's diagnosis when he examines the gowns."

"And just when will that be happening, so I can offer my *expert opinion*?"

He calmly glanced at his gold Rolex. "In approximately an hour the gowns will be delivered to his lab here. I'll be back afterward. Rest now like the doctor ordered."

Since she'd woken up in this hospital bed, her whole world felt out of rhythm, with her two beats behind. Only when Drew turned to leave the room did she think of more comebacks for his smug confidence about the dresses.

But could they be right?

Again, the memory hovered just out of reach.

She looked up to see her sisters peeking through the open door. "Swear to me you won't e-mail or phone Dad about this," Athena called out, suddenly afraid the Fates, Drew, truth serum, *and* her father were more than she could deal with at the moment.

"We swear, but we need to leave now. The doctor wants you to rest," Diana called softly.

"We'll be back in a few hours with your favorite Leonidas chocolate," Venus promised and blew a kiss.

At the precise moment of blowing a kiss back to her sisters, the nagging memory she couldn't quite grasp earlier leaped out and hit her over her head.

She'd stood in a hospital doorway blowing a kiss to T. A. Long, her favorite costume curator in the whole world, when he was in the hospital with a strange ailment after doing a thorough examination of a black Dior evening dress.

No, it can't be the same illness. T. A. was so much sicker.

Groaning, she shut her eyes, trying to figure out if the two incidents could truly be related.

T. A.'s illness had been caused by fumes from degrading plastic that designers sprayed on the netting under dresses decades ago. Could the boning in the much older Bertha Palmer dresses be degrading and have a similar effect?

Tears burned in her eyes, and she quickly brushed them away. She didn't want the Bertha Palmer gowns to be found guilty of poisoning her. She wanted them placed in the museum, where they belonged. They were tangible pieces of Chicago history for future generations to enjoy and learn from. They were the centerpiece of the exhibit that would generate enough money to cement the scholarship in her mother's honor and start Makayla on the road to a great future. If only Athena's dad hadn't dropped the ball because of the Clayworth mess, it would all be in place and none of this would have happened.

But it *had* happened, and she had to fix it.

Despite Drew Clayworth, who had the distinction of being her first really big mistake.

On the way to Lewis Stemmer's office, Drew couldn't help laughing to himself. Prim and proper Athena Smith had challenged him about knowing his way up a woman's skirt. And told him what she thought of him.

Why didn't I do the same instead of kissing her?

Did she remember it? Had it brought back any old memories for her, like it had for him?

He needed to know what game she was playing this time. Her eyes had always given her away. That's how he'd known what she'd done to him.

She didn't need those damn glasses, the same large, pale-smoke-tinted lenses, the kind shaded at the top so they're clear over the cheeks, she'd been wearing in all the newspaper pictures he'd seen of her in the last few months.

She was hiding behind them, just as Rebecca's columns hinted. Hiding her feelings about the loss of her father's spotless reputation.

The latter at the hands of his family.

Tension tightened like a vise around his neck and shoulders. He shrugged, trying to relax. He never second-guessed himself. He felt as sure of his decision about Alistair as he did Lewis Stemmer's medical diagnosis of Athena's illness.

Drew stopped in the glass walkway between the hospital and Lewis's office. Below on Superior Street, Venus and Diana were getting into a cab.

If Drew believed in fate, Athena's reappearance in his life would be some kind of omen. She'd been there on the cold, snowy night he first vowed to win the yacht race that ultimately killed his parents. And here she appeared again on the eve of his finally fulfilling his promise to himself to race in the Fastnet.

The memory of the first Christmas after his parents died rubbed painfully against his hard protective shell. He'd let her in that night, and the aftermath had changed him.

He strolled slowly, giving himself a few more minutes to stop thinking about their past. At the moment he couldn't avoid Athena, and it had nothing to do with their fate being written in the stars like she had once told him, lying on the sand at the Clayworth beach, regaling him with the myths her father had woven for her. Then he'd been totally taken in, no doubt from teenage testosterone.

He'd learned a long time ago the only thing in the heavens were the constellations that guided lost sailors at sea.

He'd confirm Lewis's diagnosis and make sure she got what she needed to get well. Clayworth's would assume all responsibility. That would be the end of it.

Decision made, he glanced at his watch and took the stairs so he wouldn't be late for the appointment with Bertha's gowns.

Connor stood waiting for him. He'd seen this look before on his face. Poised, armed, ready to do battle.

"What the hell is wrong now?" he demanded, striding in and shutting the door.

Then he saw Lewis standing over Bridget, who looked small, huddled in a chair. Ed Mahoney, Clayworth's top insurance specialist, sat beside her.

Again that edge of dread sliced through him. "Bridget, what are you doing here? You should be at home resting."

"No, I had to tell you myself." Her green eyes looked flat and dull, very different than yesterday. "Drew, the Bertha Palmer gowns are gone. All four of them. Someone's broken into the Secret Closet."

CHAPTER 4

Bridget swayed in her chair. A rush of adrenaline drove Drew toward her.

Lewis got there first and lifted her wrist in his long fingers.

She shook him off, casting them all the warning glance Drew remembered seeing a hundred times growing up. She hated any mollycoddling, as she called it.

"I'm not looney like I was yesterday. I know this is my fault. I was so worried about Athena I don't remember whether or not I set the code on the closet's small door. Then with all of us tramplin' through the place today, we probably destroyed any evidence there might have been."

Lewis nodded. "I can't tell you this isn't a problem. If I'm right, those dresses need to be found before anyone else becomes infected."

"We will, Lewis. I promise." Anger that someone would violate the Secret Closet made his voice cold. "We're all concerned about the danger to others."

"That's the problem, Drew. I'm not sure of the extent of the danger until I study the toxin. So far, exposure hasn't been life-threatening. But that could change. That threat is what we must contain. I'll notify the proper authorities and keep you informed."

They all stared at one another in silence long after Lewis left the room. They all knew Clayworth's reputation was at stake at a time when they were vulnerable.

Ed, short, bulky, and ruddy cheeked, cleared his throat like he always did before presenting them with the store's latest insurance crisis. "Until the gowns are recovered—and I'm confident they'll be found—I know you want the insurance settled. I took the liberty of bringing the necessary paperwork for the board members to sign." He laid out what looked like reams of forms.

Another kick of déjà vu. Ed looking and sounding like this on the day after Drew's parents' funeral. Sitting in Henry's three-story library in the main house of the Clayworth compound, there had been a different feel in the room. Today the family looked coiled tight, ready to take action. Then they'd been melancholy while Ed explained the huge insurance policy and Uncle Henry talked about the seventeen percent of John Clayworth and Company Drew now owned.

At nineteen he'd damned the facts and figures. Hadn't cared about the family fortune. His parents were gone. A future without them had looked long and lonely. Until Henry clasped his shoulder and Marilyn, his uncle's newest wife, gathered Drew against her ample Chanel-clad bosom, declaring they would be his new family.

He glanced around at Connor, signing papers with one hand and patting Bridget's shoulder with the other.

They'd all been there for him. The only family he had left.

Connor turned away to read a form Ed thrust into his face, and Bridget looked up at Drew. "I'm sorry I forgot to ask about Athena. Dr. Stemmer said you were with her. How is she feelin'?"

"Definitely better. My guess is that he'll release her today."

Drew glanced down at the form Ed slid in front of him, to hide his feelings from Bridget.

Athena had been there for him, too. Until the night everything changed.

He signed the last sheet and pushed it back toward Ed. "This is not going to be as simple and neat as signing insurance claims. Once we notify the police, the story will be plastered all over the media."

"Don't worry." Connor had on his lawyer face. "I can delay the media frenzy. My contact at the police department will take care of the robbery report. It will be recorded for insurance purposes and then kept securely under wraps for three weeks. If we can convince the Smith sisters to keep quiet, we've got twenty-one days to find those dresses before all hell breaks loose."

"Under those circumstances, will the police still investigate?" Drew asked.

"If there's an investigation, I'll be the number-one suspect," Bridget stated flatly.

"Aunt Bridget, you're above suspicion. Don't worry. I'll handle everything." Connor's frown shifted to the sweet, sensitive smile he reserved only for her. Drew had seen plenty of women try to coax the same smile out of Connor and fail.

If Drew weren't a master at hiding his own feelings, he would have missed the flash of guilt in Bridget's eyes.

Seeing it felt like a blade through his heart. She'd been like a mother to him. "Connor's right. No one blames you for this, Bridget."

He moved to stand beside her, shoulder to shoulder with Connor, like the Clayworths always stood.

Ed gave a deep, rumbling sigh. "I'm sure the insurance company won't consider anyone in this room a suspect in the theft. However, they may be concerned about Athena suing all of you for what happened to her there." He cleared his throat again. "I hesitate to mention this, but is it possible with Athena's connections in the vintage world that she could be involved in this theft?"

Drew's eyes clashed with Connor's, and the room rang with it.

"Think about it, Drew. Vintage couture is Athena's specialty. And the gowns were the only items taken."

Odd he felt the need to defend her. "Or someone wants us to believe Athena is involved. So this was a good time to make their move."

Fury in her eyes, Bridget pushed herself up. "This is total rubbish, and I forbid all of you to ever mention such a thing again! Those lovely young women aren't guilty of anythin' besides loathin' the lot of us."

Connor shrugged. "I agree about Diana and Athena. But I wouldn't put anything past Venus. Short of committing the robbery herself."

Bridget smiled, her eyes widening, like the thought intrigued her. Ed turned an unhealthy scarlet, obviously embarrassed to be found so far off base.

Drew knew the spirited Smith sisters were capable of a

great deal. Larceny? He doubted it. Even if their father's dealings were questionable.

"Ed, you're right about Athena's connections. She could help us locate possible black-market venues where the dresses might be sold. Lewis said we need to find those missing dresses before anyone else becomes affected. It's Clayworth's responsibility."

Connor nodded. "If you can convince Athena to keep quiet, we have three weeks to do it until we'll be in a legal tangle we don't need right now on the heels of the Alistair mess."

A ticking clock, like the Clayworth symbol crowning the corner of their flagship store in Chicago's Loop, loomed over Drew. He had three weeks to keep the others safe. Three weeks before he left for the Fastnet in England. Three weeks to deal with Athena Smith back in his life.

He had no other choice but to start now by telling her the truth and ask for her help.

"Athena, I knew I should have gone to help you no matter what." Makayla launched herself down to engulf Athena in a breath-defying hug.

Athena sucked in some air. Happy to be free of the IV bags, she patted Makayla's shoulder. "Don't upset yourself," she soothed as she'd done so often for her sisters. "I'm glad you weren't there. We certainly don't need the two of us in hospital beds. What would the museum do without us?"

"You're right. Gotta keep the place going." With a deep, shuddering sigh, Makayla pulled herself up, kohl smeared around her wet eyes. "Everyone at the museum sends their love. Leonard sent these awesome flowers from his garden."

Makayla thrust a fragrant bouquet of tiny roses toward Athena.

Thinking of gruff, rugged Leonard tending roses in the greenhouse window of his kitchen sent a rush of affection curling through her.

As if on cue, a volunteer strolled into the room, staggering a bit under the weight of an enormous bouquet of pink roses and baby's breath.

Makayla yanked her small bouquet behind her back.

The older woman smiled. "Hello, dear. We have this beautiful bouquet for you."

Athena quickly read the small white enclosure card and stopped smiling back. No rush of affection here. More like unease. It didn't feel right to take it. "Thank you, but I'm sure there are other patients on the floor who would love to have these flowers. I already have a beautiful bouquet."

Disbelief plainly written across her face, the older woman gasped. "You don't want these lovely flowers?"

Athena knew Drew had sent flowers from Clayworth's out of expediency.

"I'd like to share the flowers. I'm sure I'll be going home today," Athena said softly. She didn't want to be rude, but she hoped the woman would retreat, taking the arrangement with her.

Mercifully, she seemed to understand and backed from the room. Through the open door Athena saw her put the flowers back on the cart and clatter down the hall.

Ponytail swinging, Makayla marched forward to place

Leonard's bouquet on the bedside table. "You want this one, right?"

"Love it." Athena smiled up and caught Makayla staring at Drew lounging in the open doorway.

Of course she's staring. His air of supreme confidence always made him irresistible. Even now, when I know better.

"Is he, like, a movie star or something?" Makayla whispered, giving Drew the once-over.

"Drew Clayworth."

"For real? He's hot," she breathed, her eyes straying back to him.

Hot. Another scene drifted through her head. Her dressed in this same hideous puke green gown, throwing herself at Drew, clinging to him and smothering him in kisses. Truth, or hallucination like Bertha and Jackie?

Please, please don't let it be true.

Her stomach felt hollow, like it did when she had to do something she dreaded. She sucked up her courage to find out the truth. "I need to talk privately for a few minutes with Mr. Clayworth."

Makayla appeared not to hear her as she peered at him through half-closed lids, her cheeks rosy, her pale lips parted.

"*Makayla,*" Athena breathed, trying to be discreet.

Looking down at her with owl eyes, Makayla blinked. "Awesome. Got ya. I'll be back later."

At the door, Drew stepped aside for her to pass. "Have a good day," he said before strolling in.

He appeared totally unconscious of the nearly swooning young woman he'd left in his wake.

Some things never change.

But she'd changed. She no longer felt guilt, regret, and confusion about what she'd done so long ago. Now he had no effect on her whatsoever. Again the prickly heat crawled along her skin. Had she confessed something else when she'd thrown herself at him?

Safe behind her concealing glasses, Athena braced herself to find out.

"Why do you wear those glasses? You had Lasik surgery when you were seventeen," he said lightly.

Thrown off by his new tack, she fiddled with the frames. *What's he up to now?* "I'm having eye strain from work."

"I can give you the name of an excellent ophthalmologist."

"No, thank you. I have my own."

"Who is he?"

"*He* is a *she*." Athena thrust up her chin, wanting to get this unpleasantness over with. "I need to tell Dr. Stemmer that I've remembered one of my colleagues was hospitalized with symptoms similar to mine after examining a Dior dress. The netting was degrading and giving off toxic substances, so...so I believe something similar has happened with the boning in Bertha's gown. We must conserve the Bertha Palmer dress by placing it in cold storage. The degradation process is slowed down significantly, and then the boning can be replaced."

He nodded, and she saw him square his shoulders, like he'd always done when he needed to do something he dreaded. "We will as soon as we find the dress."

"Find the dress?" Shock brought her straight up in bed. "What are you talking about? You told me it was being delivered to the hospital hours ago."

"The closet was broken into after you left. All four Bertha Palmer dresses were taken."

His words froze her in disbelief and fear. "No! Those priceless dresses need to be safe in my museum where I can take care of them. Are there any suspects?"

Deep in his eyes, guilt flickered. She saw it and jumped to her own conclusion.

"Surely no one believes I had anything to do with this?"

His tiny pause sent such passionate anger roaring through her, she wouldn't have been surprised if smoke spewed from her ears. "Oh, my God, you *do* think I did this!"

He shook his head. "Athena—"

"You honestly think I made myself sick so someone could steal those dresses!" she out-shouted him.

"No, I..."

After all she'd been through with his family and with *him,* he didn't look contrite enough to her.

Or is this the truth serum still at work?

"I should sue you for defamation of character, even if my dad didn't!"

Again something shifted through his eyes, buried so deep in the blazing blue, but she saw it.

"Oh, my God, you think I'm actually going to sue you, too!" The injustice of being so maligned when she'd taken the high road and *not* retaliated against them consumed her in red-hot rage. She folded her arms across her heaving bosom and turned away. "Leave my room at once."

"No. I'm not leaving until we figure this out. We both want those dresses back, right?"

His strong authoritian tone instead of his usual light banter made it impossible not to respond. She glanced coolly back at him. "At last, you've said something true."

"I haven't said anything. You're the one putting words in my mouth. All I want is your promise to keep quiet about this and get your family and friends to do the same while you help me get the dresses back." He gave her his signature charming smile, the one calculated to help him get his own way.

She certainly wasn't giving in to him, but the thought of careless, cruel hands destroying Bertha's legacy to Chicago made her decide to consider his suggestion. "Do the police have any *real* suspects? Any clues? Those dresses need to be found before they're harmed."

He narrowed his eyes. "They need to be found so no one else becomes infected by them."

His rebuke stung her. Embarrassment burned through the flimsy hospital gown. "*That* goes without saying. If the thieves don't keep the dresses themselves, they'll fence them to high-end collectors."

She felt sick thinking of others enduring a headache so pounding it could surely be compared to Zeus's when, according to Greek mythology, her namesake sprang fully grown out of his skull.

If exposed, would others react like I did? Shout their secret feelings to the world?

Feelings about Drew she'd thought long dead and buried under time and maturity.

Now she needed to push all her personal feelings aside for the greater good.

And the greater good for the museum, for Chicago,

came miraculously presented to her on the proverbial Clayworth, rimmed-in-real-gold-and-sterling-silver, platter.

She pushed her glasses higher on her nose. "Since I'm the expert on the dresses and know most of the serious collectors, I can help find them. And when I do, I want them for the exhibit at the museum."

This time he lowered his lids so she couldn't read his eyes. "Since Clayworth's was founded, it has been our policy never to loan out certain family treasures. The dresses fall under that category."

"There's a first time for everything."

Their eyes met and clashed. "What's your proposition, Athena?"

Refusing to be cowed by Clayworth tradition, she lifted her chin. "I propose that we forget our personal feelings. Temporarily," she amended. "We forget everything that might have transpired between us in this hospital because of conditions beyond our control. And we work together to find the dresses, and then, as a gesture of civic goodwill, you allow them to be displayed at the museum as an important piece of our Founding Families Exhibit."

At last a flicker of genuine emotion he didn't try to hide, amusement of all things, lit his eyes.

"You've got a deal, partner."

His words rang in her ears, making her feel dizzy again. Obviously her world still beat to a different drummer than usual, or she wouldn't have just agreed to work shoulder to shoulder with the enemy.

CHAPTER 5

The phone started ringing on the oak chest beside Athena's four-poster bed, disturbing her beloved Drusilla Junior curled as usual along her right hip. Weak light filtered around the lace curtains at her bedroom window. Awake, but still groggy from "sleeping it off," as Dr. Stemmer put it, she slowly fought through her pile of fluffy pillows to reach out and pick up the phone on the fourth ring.

Drew? Her partner? The thought made her stomach growl.

No, no, she knew who it would be. Since she'd won the battle with her sisters to stay alone in her own bed, in her little piece of peace, her restored Lincoln Park carriage house, she'd expected them to check up on her at dawn.

"I love you for caring so much, but I'm just fine," she said briskly into the phone.

"Certainly I'm pleased to hear it. When you failed to

attend our meeting on Friday afternoon after you insisted on scheduling it, all I could get out of Makayla was that you had gone to the ER with a headache."

The exasperated tone of Edna Keene, deputy director of the museum, sounded all too familiar. Athena sent a silent thanks to Makayla for keeping her secret as they had all sworn to do until further notice, even with Edna breathing down her neck.

Consumed with worry over Bertha's missing dresses, Athena had let her meeting with Edna simply vanish from memory. Now it came rushing back with all its importance.

"Athena, are you still there?" Edna asked, a new irritation in her voice.

A little edge of panic made Athena fling back the covers, drop down on the cool wood floor, and begin to pace. "Yes, I'm here, just a little groggy." She needed to go eyeball to eyeball with Edna. Needed to convince her and the board to continue her dad's efforts to establish a scholarship fund. They needed to give her the green light on the exhibit.

She chose her words carefully. "I'm really sorry about the meeting. It was unavoidable. Could we please reschedule for Monday?"

"I'm in the Red Carpet Room at O'Hare. My flight to Paris leaves in ninety minutes. It will have to wait until I return from the conference in two weeks."

Athena stood rooted to a spot in front of the small brick fireplace. "Another two weeks? You stopped my work on the exhibit weeks ago. There's barely time now to complete the exhibit and plan the black tie opening."

Edna's heavy sigh sent an icy chill from Athena's curling toes to her scorching cheeks.

"Athena, I told you, since your father resigned as a trustee, enthusiasm for expanding the Chicago Founding Families Exhibit and establishing a scholarship fund has waned on the board."

"And I told you I'd find the funding myself," she snapped back, fighting off the beginnings of another dull headache. *Oh, my God, did I sleep off all the truth serum?*

"Someone got up on the wrong side of the bed this morning," Edna said in a tight little voice. "You know these things take time."

Sick at the idea of letting Makayla down, Athena turned on her heels and paced the other way. "Edna, you know Makayla doesn't have time. When she turns eighteen next month, she'll be emancipated from the foster system. She needs our help now."

The dreaded sigh again. Deeper, louder this time. She knew if she could see Edna, she'd be puffing out her thin chest and blowing through tense lips.

"Athena, your family is employing Makayla at your new emporium, which is generous of you. Do I need to remind you again that the museum is not a charity to help orphaned young ladies, no matter how gifted?"

Makayla *was* talented. She'd beat out the competition on her own merit. Athena had tried to be impartial, but inwardly she'd been rooting for her. She didn't know exactly why Makayla grabbed her around the heart, but she did, and Athena refused to fail her now.

Anger burned away her need to be diplomatic. Or maybe truthfulness had residual effects.

"Edna, my mother helped build the Costume Collection from nothing to the second best in this country," she said through clenched teeth because she shivered from the cold and frustration. "The collection has enhanced the museum's reputation enormously, which is probably why you've been asked to the conference in Paris. And let us not forget that my father, through his financial expertise, helped solidify the museum's endowment. I believe my family has earned a few minutes of your time and consideration of my request."

Edna's silence stabbed at Athena's already bruised heart. No one had actually accused her father of embezzlement within her hearing, but she'd heard the gossip many times. Had *felt* it. Like she herself felt the dull ache of anger toward her dad. Why hadn't he fought the Clayworths for his good name, or tried to explain, or even come up with an excuse? Anything would be better than his black hole of silence.

At last Edna gave another of her classic exasperated sighs. "We will discuss this upon my return."

"Yes, we will. By then I'll have the funding myself. Have a good flight." She clicked off the phone and threw it on the bed.

She *would* finish what her father had started. Nothing else mattered.

Except for the not-so-small matter of her guilt.

She didn't give a damn whether or not Drew suspected her of thievery. Maybe he'd agreed to her proposal so he could watch her. She didn't care about his motives. She'd stick to their unhealthy alliance to get what she needed.

She *did* care that her becoming ill might have compromised the Secret Closet's security system because

Bridget left it unlocked when Athena had to be rushed to the hospital. If she hadn't stuck her head under the skirt for hours, the dresses and further unsuspecting victims of the fumes might never have been at risk. So not only did she have to fix the mess her father left, she must do whatever it took to help Drew find the Bertha Palmer dresses. The sooner the better. Like sands through the hourglass, time was running out. She had less than three weeks.

She glanced at the small crystal clock on her bedside table. Saturday morning, opening day at Pandora's Box.

Fixing the past would have to wait a few more hours.

Like on most Saturday mornings, Drew walked through the heavy doors of the Chicago Athletic Union.

Absently swinging his racket bat, he plotted his next move with Athena. Could he trust her to keep up her end of things?

He took the steps two at a time to control his surge of adrenaline. He had no time for confusion. Regardless of their past, he and Athena needed to find those dresses together, and soon.

On the landing, he glanced up at the life-size paintings of his great-grandfather John Clayworth, the founder of the club, and grandfather William Clayworth, who had been the life force keeping the game of rackets flourishing in Chicago. Drew saluted them as he passed, acknowledging how well they'd kept their mission alive.

He and Connor were like all Clayworth males for generations, believing rackets was more than a ball game for two or four people played with bats and a hard ball in a high, four-walled slate court. It was a gentleman's game in which they developed the camaraderie, the

Clayworth loyalty, that the family had become legendary for maintaining.

They were as solid as ever, but a hell of a lot less gentlemanly, playing harder on and off the court.

Ducking, Drew stepped through the short steel door into one of three racket courts still remaining at the club.

"You're late!" Connor called out.

"I'm still taking your money this morning," Drew laughed, swinging his bat.

He glanced up into the galley to make sure Patrick, the rackets pro, hadn't arrived yet to be their marker before they discussed family business. "Whoever wins decides whether or not we attend the opening of Pandora's Box today."

"Are you nuts? Did you get a whiff of that truth serum? They've agreed to keep quiet about the dresses. Let's not give them reason to change their minds." Connor didn't disguise his impatience. "As Clayworth legal counsel, I advise against it."

"Cut the lawyer crap, Connor. You know as well as I do that Ann Smith was Henry's muse for years. She helped make the Fashions of the Hour Shop what it is today. The fact her daughters hate our guts doesn't change anything. I told you Athena and I cut a deal. Besides, you're the one who told me I needed to keep communication open with her."

"I say we leave it alone." Connor locked eyes with him, and their war of wills filled the room with tension. "If we attend, the speculation about Alistair's retirement will start up again."

"It's never gone away." Drew glanced up. "Patrick is here. Let's play."

His mind more on the reason for the tight band of tension between them than on the game, Drew let Connor take the point.

With each slam of his bat, and each point Patrick called out above them, Drew watched Connor and thought about Alistair Smith. So highly trusted by Clayworth's for decades. What had gone wrong?

Could the missing dresses have anything to do with Alistair? Could Athena be involved?

Drew served hard to the corner, and Connor missed the shot.

Connor shook his head. "All right. I owe you a twenty, but you haven't won yet."

Drew nodded, but he couldn't concentrate on the game. He kept thinking how Connor saw the world in black and white. To Connor, Alistair had been duplicitous and responsible for major losses at their bottom line. Did he see Athena in the same way?

Again, Drew went through his analysis of the case against Alistair. The investments gone wrong. They had been significant, but not fatal. When had Alistair decided to become a gambler, making riskier investments, trying for bigger returns to cover his losses?

Did Athena know Drew's had been the deciding vote condemning her father and demanding he step down?

If Alistair wasn't the one to sign off on the risky investments, it had to be one of my cousins.

The ball whizzed past Drew's ear.

He needed to get his head back in the game, not dwell on the impossible.

He hit Connor's next serve neat and perfect, and the game escalated into a battle of wills. The slam of the ball against the wall over and over again became the rhythm of the pure male aggression rising off them like sweat. Christ, they hadn't played with this much concentration in championship games. No banter, just blood-and-guts competition. Forget their usual bets. Today it was all about the Smith sisters, their dad, and, for Drew, the past.

He needed to get this over with. He hit the ball hard to Connor, slamming in the winning point.

Breathing and sweating like stallions after a race, their white shirts hanging out and white shorts rumpled and creased, they both bent over, catching their breath.

Drew caught his first. "We go to Pandora's Box. I talk to Athena. Then I'm taking the kids from the center sailing before my race."

Connor looked up at him and frowned. "You're racing a lot lately. What's going on?"

Drew shrugged. "You know I love it. Clayworths are creatures of habit. Look at us."

Connor laughed. "Yes. Sometimes I hate this game."

Drew nodded. "Yeah, I hear you. On that note, I'm heading for a shower."

Connor followed him. "What's bothering you, Drew? Are you second-guessing yourself about Athena? Do you think they're up to something?"

Some emotion Drew couldn't put a name to swept through him. "I don't know yet. Today is about paying our debt to Ann Smith for years of loyalty by supporting her daughters in a new business enterprise." *Yeah, and an excuse to see Athena to figure the rest out.*

Connor walked away but turned back to flash one of his rare grins. "For the record, I think you're up to something. If you ever need me to crew for you, I'm in."

Drew slowly followed him into the locker room, feeling guilty about keeping his plans to himself.

Yeah, he was up to something. Bridget had been right. It was more than time for him to fix himself. Finally fulfill the promise he'd made to himself. A promise Athena had stopped him from keeping.

Standing in the shower, letting the hot water pound over his shoulders, Drew couldn't stop thinking about Athena. Trying like he had a hundred times before to understand why she'd betrayed his trust. He'd told her about that first time in Cowes on the Isle of Wight in England, standing with his parents as the competitors set sail on the famous offshore yachting race—the excitement he'd felt. Forty-four hours and eighteen minutes later, when the winner sailed into Plymouth in the South of England, after rounding the Fastnet Rock off the southwest coast of Ireland, they were there to see it. The passion to be that winner burned in his gut. He'd told his parents he wanted to race in the Fastnet. Knew they could win it.

He'd explained it all to Athena, his best friend. Why had she lied and said she understood?

Closing his eyes, Drew turned his face up and let the water cascade over it. It reminded him of the two years he'd been away from Chicago, away from everyone he cared about, to sail with his mom and dad while they perfected their skills for the next Fastnet race. They'd raced through sparkling swells that tossed back a spritzing of spray and towering black mountains of water that drenched him. He had been as good a sailor as both of them, better, in fact, and they knew it.

Yet they still wouldn't let him crew the Fastnet, even

though it had been his desire driving them from the beginning.

Drew turned on the cold water, numbing the memory of that last day when he'd begged them to let him go with them. He could still see his father's stern face telling him they had decided it was too dangerous. Feel his mother's cool lips on his cheek as she whispered, *You're so young, sweetie. All the crews are older and very experienced sailors.*

Experience hadn't been enough when the killer gale smashed through the 303-boat fleet off the English and Irish coasts, leaving fifteen dead, five boats sunk, and another seventy-five capsized. His parents dead from something he suggested they do.

He hadn't been a kid for a very long time. Back then, he'd been irrational, thinking he could have changed it all if he'd been allowed to go.

He knew his racing in the Fastnet wouldn't bring his parents back, wouldn't change the outcome. Yet he needed to do it to assuage his feelings of guilt and regret. It represented closure for him, and he knew it was more than time for him to find it.

"Hey, what the hell are you doing in there? Leave some water for the next guy! I'm in the bar waiting for you," Connor shouted and rapped on the glass shower door.

Drew shut off the water, wrapped a towel around his hips, and stepped out. "Sorry. I'll join you in a few minutes."

Connor studied him through narrow eyes. "Tell me what's eating you. Do you want me to work with Athena on this instead of you?"

Drew shrugged. "I'm fine. Thinking too much about paying debts."

"Clayworths always do, with interest. Why else would you want us to risk the wrath of Athena and her sisters?" Connor walked away, leaving Drew staring after him.

Athena, who owed him a debt. Was it time for her to pay?

Athena owed it to her sisters, who were hovering around her, to have ignored Edna's dawn phone call. This was supposed to be one of the happiest days of their lives, and Athena would make it that and more. If only Venus weren't determined to give her another headache.

"I still think the moment Rebecca arrives to tape the segment for *Talk of the Town,* we should tell her what happened to you at Clayworth's Secret Closet," Venus declared for the third time.

Diana rose, quivering in fury, and placed her hands on her narrow hips. Even though Diana stood only five foot one and one half inches in her bare feet and Venus five foot seven in hers, they seemed to be glaring eyeball to eyeball. Sometimes Athena thought Diana's strong will made her taller when necessary.

"Absolutely not, Venus! I absolutely forbid it!" Diana shouted.

Makayla looked around from where she fussed, perfectly adjusting the heavy velvet drapery to the dressing room, and frowned.

Athena threw her an encouraging smile and stepped between her sisters. "Diana is right. You agreed to the deal I made with Drew for Bertha's dresses."

"I know, and I understand why you did it, Athena, but

I'll never understand why Diana continues to work for their stores and, worse, actually defends the Clayworths." Venus leveled her powerful glare upon their tiny sister, who, as usual, refused to flinch.

"I have my reasons," Diana retorted, again refusing to discuss her decision not to resign her position as director of window displays and interior decoration for all ten stores.

Wanting to set a good example for Makayla, who obviously couldn't resist her urge to eavesdrop, Athena adopted her older-sister voice. "Venus, you know as well as I do the Clayworths begged and offered Diana more money than they should have to stay in her position."

Venus threw a rope of her hair over one shoulder and sniffed with disdain. "Some people are willing to sell their souls to the devil. I can't believe it of my baby sister."

"Please!" Diana drawled. "You'd sell your soul for a vintage Kenneth Jay Lane piece."

"Only if it was signed," Venus snapped.

"Exactly," Athena sighed, negotiating for cool-down time. "Venus, you're a genius with jewelry. Diana is a display genius who can do more with accessories, fabric, and trimmings than anyone in Chicago. Look what she's done with Pandora's Box."

The two rooms reminded Athena of the inside of a velvet jewelry box. This main room, all soft pink and brown, flowed into the smaller one, dominated by a ladies' art deco vanity table with a triple mirror. A more perfect setting didn't exist for customers to try on hats or delight in exquisite toilette items. Compacts, crystal perfume bottles, hair receivers, sterling silver and ivory comb-and-brush sets were all perfectly displayed, along with one-of-a-kind purses and hand-sewn gloves.

Venus shrugged. "I love you, Diana, but I'll never truly understand your decision to stay on there after the unjust way they treated Dad."

Guilt made Athena look away.

Loving Venus, if you only knew how confused I am about the Clayworths, you wouldn't understand me, either.

A commotion outside the door swung them all toward it, releasing the little ribbon of tension twisting around them.

Rebecca Covington-Sumner, dazzling in a red Valentino suit, swept in, followed by her cameraman. "Darlings, you all look beautiful, as usual!"

Rebecca blew a kiss to Makayla, who stood timidly by the counter, hugged Venus and Diana, and stepped in front of Athena, staring intently through the tinted glasses.

Athena had the unsettling feeling that the truly wise Rebecca could see right into her eyes and thoughts. Since Dad's trouble, Rebecca had been even more extraordinarily kind.

"Darling! Why were you in the hospital overnight? No one will talk."

Athena knew if Rebecca had *really* probed deeper, someone at the hospital would have gossiped. People always told her everything.

"Just some silly bug." She squeezed Rebecca's hands and stepped back to twirl around. Her black dress—Dior New Look, 1940s—swirled around her knees. "See? All better. Today is much too special to miss."

"Your mother would be so proud," Rebecca sighed, sharing her sweet smile with all of them.

Diana blinked her long lashes, as if trying to ward off tears.

"No getting weepy. Even happy tears. Or I will, too," Rebecca scolded gently. "Can't have all of us with red noses and running mascara on television." She turned around, surveying the room. "Phil, I want shots of the store, and then I'll do the interviews before the hordes of customers start pouring in."

"Here's hoping," Venus laughed, glancing lovingly at the table of exquisite vintage costume jewelry and semi-precious jewelry she'd collected.

"Phil, on my cue, please get a shot of those costume pieces on the right and the semiprecious on the left of that table," Rebecca ordered and adjusted her microphone.

"I'm ready on three," she said softly. She took a long, deep breath. "One . . . two . . . three." Rebecca looked straight at the camera, and her smile was so warm and welcoming it lit up the store.

No wonder *Talk of the Town* was such a hit.

"Good morning, darlings! Up and at it this beautiful Chicago spring day. As promised, we are here at the grand opening of Pandora's Box, the Smith sisters' fabulous vintage emporium. You all remember this was once the home of LuLu's at the Belle Kay, until the divine owner, Laurie, won the biggest lotto in history. A longtime family friend of the Smiths, Laurie passed on to them the mantle of providing the most exquisite vintage couture in Chicago. Then off she went for a five-year around-the-world shopping holiday with her handsome husband on their fabulous yacht. When last sighted, they were in Monte Carlo and looked absolutely marvelous. Laurie is planning to send treasures to the Smith sisters from the finest closets in the world. So frequent visits to Pandora's Box are a must."

At the barely perceptible flutter of Rebecca's hand, with its huge five-karat diamond ring, Phil panned to the large, round jewelry table.

"Speaking of treasures, my name is on that simple but sensational necklace with the deep green pools of emeralds. Tell me about this piece, Venus."

"You have a great eye for the best, Rebecca. It's a rare, 1952 Christian Dior Paris necklace. Simplistic silhouette, but the green paste emeralds and diamantes set in sterling are captivating. It's one of the best pieces in the store." Venus picked it up as if they'd rehearsed.

Pride swelled in Athena's chest as she watched Venus show off her expertise in jewelry and Diana displayed her first collectable piece, a 1930 white microbeaded purse with a gold frame encrusted with diamantes, and had Makayla model a jaunty little black velvet evening hat. Athena felt their mother beside her and gave silent thanks to her for intuitively knowing each of their passions and guiding them into the fabulous world of vintage fashion, the way Athena now wanted to help Makayla.

The vision of the black velvet gown Athena had seen in a vintage store as a teenager and rushed in to purchase floated into her memory. She loved the low-cut bodice encrusted with jet, the puffy leg-of-mutton sleeves, and, best of all, the graceful train. She remembered finding the finger loop for the train and using it, dancing around the dressing room, feeling like a goddess. Even though it was black, she'd vowed to be married in the dress. Long ago, young and foolish, she'd thought she would wear it for Drew.

Now it hung in her closet at the museum. Never worn, and perhaps it never would be.

The black dress morphed into a vision of her and Drew finding the four exquisite Bertha Palmer gowns crumpled in a huge heap on some thief's grimy floor.

No doubt the vision symbolized their past relationship.

Rebecca touched her shoulder, and Athena came back to the real world. "Tell me, Athena, what is the most amazing dress in Pandora's Box at the moment?"

Athena flashed the camera her best curator smile and moved to one of the closets without doors. "Without a doubt it is this 1960 Valentino." She held up the dress so the cameraman could get a good shot. "It's ivory duchesse satin with long sleeves encrusted with rhinestones. It's worn with a sleeveless matching evening coat and this belt with a beautiful rhinestone-encrusted buckle."

"Love it," Rebecca sighed, her eyes wide with admiration. "Absolutely perfect for any bride."

Rebecca gestured to the cameraman, who panned the entire store and came back to her face. "Pandora's Box is so full of delights, all you fashionistas out there won't know what to buy first!"

"Cut, Phil." Rebecca sighed. "Wonderful stuff. I'll interview the first few customers, and then we'll be out of your way."

Rebecca broke off, drawing in a short, sharp breath. Athena looked up and did the same.

Their hair still wet from showers, Drew and Connor strolled through the door.

She couldn't take her eyes off Drew, and he'd been staring at her from the moment he sauntered into the store.

Why are they here? This isn't part of our deal.

Speechless with surprise, she tore her gaze away from Drew and looked at Rebecca for help.

With a dazzling smile, Rebecca leaped into the breach. On her cue, the cameraman began to film.

"Checking out the competition, gentlemen?" Rebecca laughed up at them.

With legendary Clayworth charm, Drew's cornflower gaze swept over Rebecca, from her Christian Louboutins to her halo of light hair, as he slowly smiled. "Pandora's Box is the place to be today. Especially with you here, Rebecca."

Rebecca gave him a knowing glance. "Ah, Drew, always the charmer."

He grinned. "We're also here because John Clayworth and Company has always valued other fine retailers."

"Spoken like the founder himself," Rebecca said with a laugh and moved on to Connor.

He blushed to the roots of his thick, coal-black hair, his green eyes from his father's family darkening to a deep emerald. As always, his powerful muscles seemed to be fighting his preppy clothes. "I'm picking out a gift for my aunt."

Rebecca turned away to interview the first customer coming through the door, and in three strides Drew stood at Athena's side.

"You look flushed. How are you? Still feeling any effects?"

She'd felt perfectly fine before they arrived, but now

her skin tingled with warmth. Maybe she should turn on the air conditioner in the store. It must be getting hotter outside. Bright sunlight bathed the crowd gathered on the sidewalk, drawn by the red Ferrari F430 convertible and the silver Porsche.

"Athena, are you feeling all right?" he asked again, more sharply this time.

"I'm perfectly fine." She thrust up her chin, prepared for whatever the Fates planned to deal her this time. She felt the tension vibrating off Venus, saw the curiosity in Diana's eyes and the intent way Makayla watched them all.

"Why are you really here, Drew?" She held her breath, hoping he wouldn't mention her father, the elephant in the room by his absence. Dad was represented only by the spectacular arrangement of three dozen sterling silver roses he had sent to congratulate them on the opening. If Drew said one word about their dad, all hell would break loose with Venus and Diana.

"We're here out of respect for your mother."

She *almost* believed him, but she knew there must be more to this visit. But thank goodness his words were enough to cause Diana to nod and Venus to relax.

All at once she felt furry warmth around her ankles and looked down at Drusilla Junior brushing against her.

Drew laughed, a shadow of mockery on his face. "No. This can't be. It can't be your cat from when we were kids." His eyes crinkling at the corners, he looked at Athena and then down at the cat, who promptly deserted her to rub against Drew's calf.

Smiling, he swept Junior up in his arms, and the disloyal hussy licked his hand.

His long fingers slowly stroking Drusilla's stomach mesmerized Athena. She shook her head to clear it of such foolishness and then nodded. "Of course this isn't Drusilla Senior. It's Junior, from Drusilla's first litter."

She'd forgotten how Drew's eyes seemed warmed from inside when he *really* smiled.

"Junior? Athena, I believe it's my duty to tell you this is a female."

Drew rubbed Junior under the chin, and Athena heard the cat purr loud and clear.

"Of course I know Junior is a girl. I happen to be a big fan of the designer Carolina Herrera, who has a daughter, Carolina Junior, so I did the same."

"I guess it makes sense," Drew laughed, nestling Junior in the crook of his arm.

Her beloved cat stared at her for a second, as if debating whether or not staying nestled in Drew's arm could be worth risking her treats for the day. Smart like her mother, Junior jumped daintily down to walk back to her bed in the store office, an opulent bower with the computer hidden in an antique cherry cabinet.

She looked back at Drew and caught him watching her in such an odd, intent way, she couldn't stop the heat curling through her. No doubt she blushed like the teenager she'd been the last time he'd looked at her like this.

She mustered up some cool thoughts that had nothing to do with him. "What?"

"Drusilla Junior brings back a lot of memories." His voice sounded so intimate and deep she could drown in it.

Poking her in the ribs, Venus threw her a life preserver.

"Athena, the cameraman is still filming. We should do something," she whispered.

The room came into focus, filled with curious spectators from outside wandering into the store, followed by a dozen more. Venus happily rushed off to help them.

"I'll get out of your way," Drew said in that same deep, intimate voice. "Lewis sent out an alert to all the hospitals and physicians in the area. I have Ed investigating. Anything from your contacts?"

Nothing was more important to her than finding those dresses, but for the next few hours she had to put the search on hold for Pandora's Box. "Nothing yet. I'll be in touch." Maintaining her outward calm, she nodded and walked away to help a woman looking at evening gowns.

She refused to acknowledge the memories Drew stirred, with or without Drusilla in his arms. To stop them, she threw herself into answering every question asked about vintage dresses in such detail most customers got a glazed look of information overload.

She took a deep breath, turning to find her next victim, and saw Connor waiting patiently at the counter.

He placed a gold Panetta bangle, set with beautiful green cabochon stones, in front of Venus. Even from where Athena stood, she heard Venus make a sound not quite a snort. Connor looked at her with a puzzled quirk of his lips, which Venus completely ignored.

"For my aunt Bridget," he explained.

It *was* the perfect gift for Bridget. Athena breathed a sigh of relief when, with a toss of her hair, Venus nodded and allowed Connor to buy it.

Athena deliberately looked away when Connor joined Drew and the Clayworth men made their grand exit.

Rebecca seemed to be everywhere. Smiling, enchanting

the customers, and generally making Pandora's Box the place to be today.

"How can we thank you?" Athena asked when the crowd had thinned and, to her great relief, emotionally anyway, the expensive cars had disappeared from in front of the store.

"Thank me? Darling, thank you!" Rebecca embraced her in a quick hug. "I've stayed much too long but I couldn't resist. The Clayworths and the Smiths together again is the juiciest story I've had in weeks." She sighed. "Have you ever seen better-looking men in your life—besides my David? Devastating, and both bachelors! I can hardly wait for each of them to finally meet his match. Don't forget to watch my show tomorrow morning."

With a mischievous smile, Rebecca swept out.

CHAPTER 6

On Sunday, bleary-eyed from lack of sleep, Athena perched on her large blue velvet antique settee in the sitting room of her carriage house. Well, really, how could she sleep a wink when she knew Rebecca must be up to something and Athena had made a deal with the devil? Well, Drew wasn't the devil. Worse. He continued to be the source of her misery. No, no, not misery. Disillusionment. Disappointment.

Oh, for goodness' sake, just stop thinking about him.

She tried to focus on the buildup to *Talk of the Town* as her sisters sprawled around her, sipping Veuve Clicquot mimosas to celebrate the spectacular opening of Pandora's Box.

The show's catchy theme song shocked Athena's heavy eyelids back open.

"Here it comes," Diana breathed, turning up the volume with the remote.

The second Athena heard Rebecca say, "Good morning, darlings!" her heart thumped against her ribs.

What is Rebecca going to do, and how will it impact my deal with Drew?

She tried to concentrate on how beautiful her sisters looked on TV and how sure of themselves they sounded. Best of all, Pandora's looked like a jewel box of delights, just as they'd hoped.

When the show broke for a commercial, Athena took a deep breath into her starving lungs. Until then she hadn't realized she'd barely been breathing.

Venus groaned. "I dressed to show off my jewelry. Do my new Marc Jacobs skirt and top make me look fat?"

"You aren't fat!" her long-suffering sisters shouted in unison.

Athena knew Venus had been battling her sweet tooth since she turned three and grew tall enough to climb on a chair to get to the cookie jar.

"Good. Then I can have more of this." Smiling, Venus topped off her freshly squeezed orange juice with more champagne.

Athena guzzled a bit more champagne than she should have herself, trying to cool the hot ache of anticipation boiling in her stomach.

The instant Rebecca came back onscreen, looking at the camera in such a "girlfriends telling secrets" way, Athena knew the moment had come.

"Here's a fun, sexy quiz for you." Rebecca smiled. "Who are the two outrageously wealthy, impossibly attractive, brilliant, exciting renaissance men who attended the grand opening of Pandora's Box? I'll give you a few clues. One teaches sailing to underprivileged teens, and one is a mentor to juvenile defendants. One owns adorable dogs. And as you will soon see, one has a way with cats."

Rebecca shook her head, and her sleek blond hair fell charmingly around her small ears. "I know, darlings, they sound too good to be true. And much too interesting to keep you guessing until next week. So here they are."

Athena sucked in the same sharp, short breath she had yesterday when the Clayworth men strolled into the store. She couldn't take her eyes off Drew as he walked toward the camera and Phil had panned to the two of them. Drew stroking Drusilla Junior, gazing at Athena and her gazing right back, as if they were alone in the room. She'd read about out-of-body experiences. Surely seeing and feeling the attraction to Drew all over again came close to one.

In the interest of nondisclosure, she ignored the stunned looks her sisters threw her and concentrated on what Rebecca was saying.

"Yes, you've guessed it. Drew Clayworth and his cousin Connor O'Flynn, the perennial most eligible men in Chicago." The camera panned on each of their sensual faces.

Athena had purposely not watched them leave, but the cameraman had caught it on tape. Drew paused at the door to look back. For some reason, his face relaxed and his lips curled in the briefest of smiles before he turned and left. A rush of hot curiosity made her shiver. She had the oddest wish to know what or who had made him happy. Once, long ago, she'd believed she had the power to do that.

"I've told you that Pandora's Box is dedicated to the

Smith sisters' late mother, Ann. You might know Athena, Venus, and Diana owe their unusual names to their father, Alistair's, passion for Roman and Greek goddess mythology. I'm sure our darling Smith sisters were told about Plato's claim that our earliest ancestors were born hermaphroditic and so powerful they threatened the gods, who punished them by cleaving each being in half. From then on, Plato said humans have longed for their other half, and when one finds it, love happens. I can't wait to see these commitment-phobic Clayworth men meet their better halves."

Rebecca's mischievous smile lit up the screen. "Remember, if you can't keep a secret, tell me. I always change the names to protect the guilty. The innocent don't need protecting. See you next week, darlings!"

Athena couldn't turn off the television fast enough. "Well, that was lovely. I'll go fix brunch."

"Hey, wait a minute!" Venus called after her. Curiosity blazed in her eyes. "What was that between you and Drew? You both looked mesmerized by each other."

Always a pro at hiding the truth about Drew, Athena laughed. "There is nothing *mesmerizing* about my deal with Drew. Maybe he was mesmerized by Junior."

Hearing her name, Junior looked up from licking her paws and pranced over to rub against Athena before settling in Diana's lap.

She stroked her and stared up at Athena from the floor. "I remember the summer you broke your ankle and had to stay off it for months. Every weekend we were at the Clayworth estate swimming at their private beach, Drew stayed on the sand, reading with you. I always thought you were more than friends, different than the rest of us.

What happened? All of a sudden it was like you didn't know each other."

Athena shrugged away the bitter memories. "He's a Clayworth. Obviously he can't even commit to a friendship."

Diana gazed up at her with a fey sort of knowledge beyond her years. "Drew was always different than the others."

Venus sprawled on the settee, her apricot hair falling out of its untidy topknot. "Drew is certainly different than his cousin Connor. Drew is gorgeous and charming, while Connor is so uptight I don't know how he moves without squeaking. I shudder for their better halves if they ever find them. Actually, I remember Dad telling us about Plato's theory, but I don't know how I feel about it. What if you were attracted to someone you loathed? Knew he was absolutely the worst person on the planet for you, but every time you saw him you wanted to rip his clothes off?"

"Or if you were torn between two men and loved both of them." Diana's large eyes glistened in her small face. "What do you think, Athena?"

I found him too young, and he walked away from me.

To get off the hook, she laughed. "I think Venus is too hard on Connor. Yes, he can be a bit stiff at times. But he's an absolute doll with his aunt Bridget, and she adores him, so he must have *some* redeeming qualities."

Venus laughed and threw the exquisitely embroidered pillow of bright red poppies at Athena. "All right. I admit that. But both Drew and Connor are full of themselves, so I don't feel sorry for the poor little rich men. Connor's mother is one of the biggest snobs in Chicago, but, sure, Bridget is an original. Drew?" She shrugged. "He's always been the enigma. Still waters run deep and all of that. Back me up here, Athena."

Both her sisters looked at her.

They have no idea Drew was my first love. Lately, memories of her secret, scary, sexy feelings for Drew flashed through her mind. She knew she looked flushed. Could feel the warmth seeping through her pores. Always it had been her giveaway around Drew. Her fighting the forbidden attraction.

It terrified her to be doing the same thing again. Almost like a second chance. Like the movie *Peggy Sue Got Married.* Go back and redo it. Go back and get hurt again.

Her phone rang, and they all three looked at it.

"It's Dad," Diana gasped, closest to the caller ID. "Something's wrong. He always e-mails."

"It's about time he called," Venus retorted. "When he didn't show up for the opening, I was ready to fly to Palm Beach and knock down his door to talk to him."

On the third ring, Athena picked it up and put it on the speaker. "Hi, Dad. We missed you yesterday."

But what if he had showed up? What would he have done when confronted by Connor and Drew? Been defensive, or guilty? She wished again for the hundredth-plus time that she knew why he wouldn't talk to her about what happened at Clayworth's.

"I assume you girls are all together watching *Talk of the Town.* I'm very proud of all of you." His voice sounded strong, normal, loving.

"Thanks, Dad. When are you coming home?" Venus shouted.

"Yes, we miss you tons," Diana called.

"I miss all of you, too. I'm working on some projects. I'll be there soon enough. Athena, why are you wearing those glasses? You haven't needed them in years."

Because if I wasn't, everyone could read my confusion about you and now Drew.

She fiddled with the rims, avoiding her sisters' questioning looks. "Some eye strain at work. I'll be fine."

"Make sure you take care of yourself. I love you all, and I'll see you soon. I promise."

"Love you, Dad," they chorused in unison.

Love you, Dad, but why won't you confide in me?

For the last six years since her mom died, Athena had been his confidante.

All these years, I've never told him about Drew and how he changed my life.

The truth made her sway a little on the balls of her feet. Now she had even more secrets to keep.

Diana rose as gracefully as a ballerina from the deep blue and crimson Oriental rug. "What's wrong, Athena? Are you upset about Dad's call?"

"I'm fine. Really." She shook off guilt enough to smile. "Maybe we should fly down to Florida to see him. But I just can't right now. I need to stay here and find Bertha's dresses. If I hadn't gotten sick, Bridget would have set the lock and maybe the dresses wouldn't have been stolen. Other people wouldn't run the chance of being infected."

Venus grimaced. "No way is this your fault. There are probably millions of people who have it in for the high and mighty Clayworths. They should count themselves lucky you want to help."

Diana nodded. "Totally not your fault. But you're the perfect person to help them. You have connections. Know the collectors."

She nodded. "I need those dresses for the museum. The exhibition will save the scholarship program and help Makayla." Determination burned in her blood. "I'll work with Drew to find those dresses, no matter what it costs me."

Her sisters' eyes locked, and for once she could see they were in agreement. Even to her own ears, the note of passion in her voice had been clear.

Deep inside her, fear took root. Yes, her passion to find Bertha's dresses burned brighter than ever, but heaven help her, did it still rage as hot for Drew Clayworth?

CHAPTER 7

On Monday morning at her office, fully recovered from telling the truth—at least, she *hoped* so, for everyone's sake—she called Penelope Knowles, the best-known collector of Bertha Palmer gowns in the city.

Her maid answered. "Knowles residence."

"Hi, Betty. It's Athena Smith. Is Penelope in?"

"Hello, Miss Smith. I'm sorry, Mrs. Knowles isn't home. She has a Service Club luncheon in the Maple Room at Clayworth's. May I take a message?"

"Please ask her to call me at my office or on my cell as soon as possible. She knows the numbers. Thanks, Betty."

Athena glanced at the clock. Eleven-fifteen. Did she want to wait? *Could* she wait?

She needed to find Bertha's dresses. For her mother's scholarship fund. For Makayla. For posterity. Find them to assuage her guilt for any part she may have played in getting them stolen in the first place.

Outside the museum, she hailed a cab.

Ten minutes later she walked into Chicago's retail jewel, John Clayworth and Company. Ever since she was a little girl Athena had loved shopping here, but today she was a woman on a mission. *Couture history and innocent lives are at stake here!*

She'd take up her position at the entrance to the Maple Room so Penelope couldn't escape her. Every instinct screamed that Penelope would be the first collector contacted by any legitimate seller or thief. She had a reputation for paying top dollar for what she wanted.

For an instant Athena thought she might be hallucinating again, but no, she *did* hear Penelope singing.

Athena ran down the wide aisle toward the Shoe Salon, following Penelope's loud, actually very melodious rendition of "The Lady Is a Tramp."

A crowd had formed in a tight circle, but she pushed through to the front to see a white, pleated Oscar de la Renta blouse sail past to land on a display of Brian Atwood stilettos.

Shock rooted Athena to the Clayworth blue carpet as Penelope shimmied out of her beige skirt.

"The... lady...," Penelope belted out, "is... a... tramp!"

On the last note Penelope twirled around, right into Drew's arms.

Totally ignoring the gaping crowd, he held Penelope, clad in nothing but a nude demi-bra and matching boy shorts, while he stripped off his blue button-down shirt and draped it around her.

Adrenaline rushing, Athena stumbled over shoes littering the carpet, forgotten by enthralled spectators, to fight her way to his side.

Eyes blazing, he mumbled to her, "Stay right here."

Not a minute later, Bridget led in the paramedics.

Penelope singing, "Jim, my wonderful Jim," went willingly onto the stretcher and out the door.

Drew glanced down at Athena, speechless, at his side. "I believe we have our first lead," he drawled while shrugging into a fresh shirt brought by Bridget.

Not a moment too soon. Most of the hordes of women still hovering in the shoe department were staring at his lightly golden chest and six-pack abs leading down to his low-slung jeans.

So am I.

She shook off the heady sensation of small, rippling waves of excitement to find her voice and her common sense. "We need to get to the hospital. Now."

Lewis Stemmer waited for them at the third-floor nurses' station.

"Mrs. Knowles is coherent, and her vitals are good. I explained what happened to her and asked if she'd been exposed to any of the missing Bertha Palmer dresses. She keeps insisting she bought the dress to conserve it and give it to the museum. I explained that you had suffered a similar illness from the same source. She's demanding to see you. Are you willing?" Dr. Stemmer asked.

Stricken with guilt for whatever part, even innocently, she'd played in making Penelope ill, Athena nodded. "Of course I will. Where is she?"

Drew by her side, Athena followed Dr. Stemmer to the end of the hall, where he stopped in front of a closed door.

"I believe Mrs. Knowles will be fine in a few hours."

A smile quirked Dr. Stemmer's long mouth. "Physically. The rest I hope you can help her work out. Good luck."

Adjusting her dark glasses, Athena opened the door.

Penelope Knowles lay prostrate in the bed, her arms flung out in abandonment, a cold compress across her eyes. Water leaked into her long chestnut hair, which hung limp around her face.

"Penelope, it's Athena Smith," she called softly from the foot of the bed.

"Thank God you've come," Penelope groaned and flung the cloth to the floor. Tears hanging on her lashes, mascara smeared around her eyes, Penelope stared up from the pile of pillows. "I want you to know I purchased the Bertha Palmer gown to donate to the museum. You should also know I've never done anything so reckless before, but the gown was impossible to resist, so I wore it. I know you understand, since you did the same."

Confronted by every costume curator's nightmare, Athena swallowed back her gasp of disbelief. "I didn't exactly *wear* the gown," she demurred.

"No?" Penelope lifted one finely arched brow. "Dr. Stemmer told me you suffered a similar reaction. What happened? I must know."

She identified with the real distress in Penelope's eyes and wanted to be as truthful as possible without adding to it. "After examining the gown, I began to hallucinate. I thought Bertha Palmer had come to life for a visit with me."

"Nothing else? You didn't, shall we say, expose yourself in any scandalous way?" Penelope asked, an edge of panic in her voice.

All she remembered was attacking Drew Clayworth

and revealing feelings she'd planned to take to the grave. Obviously, the truth serum affected everyone slightly differently.

But she knew what Penelope needed to hear. "I'm afraid I behaved rather foolishly."

"Foolish?" Penelope gasped. "I made a complete and utter ass out of myself in the middle of Clayworth's. I'm mortified! I'll never live this down."

Athena felt Penelope's pain. They had both made fools out of themselves. Plus Athena had reopened a painful wound that had never fully healed.

Wanting to comfort her, Athena patted Penelope's shoulder. "We're in this together."

"I knew you'd understand. I'm not totally ruined? When the gossip starts, you'll make sure people know I was under the influence of a dangerous toxic matter?" Penelope's voice caught in a sob.

Worried about the truly stricken look on her face, Athena nodded and leaned closer. "I promise. Together we'll make sure this doesn't happen to anyone else. Did you purchase all four Bertha Palmer gowns?"

Penelope's eyes widened. "My dear, the one I purchased cost a fortune, even with the tax deduction I'll receive once I donate it to the museum."

Disappointment burned a hole in Athena's already heaving stomach. "Where is the gown now?"

"In the dressing room at my condo. Dear God!" Penelope gasped. "It hasn't infected my entire wardrobe, has it? I have a divine new Lanvin I plan to wear to the Lincoln Park Zoo Ball."

"Did the gown brush against any of your other clothes?"

"No, thank God." Penelope closed her eyes. An instant later she lifted her lids and her eyes had a little of their old steely glint. "What should we do about this horror?"

"If you'll allow Drew Clayworth and me to retrieve the gown, you can put this whole unfortunate episode behind you."

"I'll call Betty immediately. She'll let you into my condo. I won't forget this, Athena," Penelope declared with real feeling. "I'll be away for a while. I'm going to Hawaii to visit my ex-husband, Jim. I plan to throw myself at his feet and beg his forgiveness. I should never have left him. I wanted my career as a cabaret singer so desperately I couldn't think of anything or anyone else. I couldn't see the truth."

"You have a lovely voice," Athena said, meaning it.

"I know, but now I understand I can have a singing career and my husband. Which I plan to do," she sighed, looking content for the first time in years.

"Thank you, Penelope. Rest easy now, and safe travels." Athena backed out of the room.

In the hallway, Drew stood waiting for her. He reached out and then quickly dropped his hands back to his sides. She had the oddest feeling he wanted to rip off her glasses.

She stuck them firmly back into place, high on her nose. "Penelope has only one of the gowns. It's in her condo on Lake Shore Drive."

Drew nodded. "Lewis says she's well enough for Connor to question her about the fence who sold it to her. That fence probably had all four dresses. What now?"

I'm a lady on a mission.

"We stop at my office for supplies, and then we go save Bertha's gown."

Betty opened the door to Penelope's condo, and the foyer light reflected off the marble floor to fall into the large rooms, decorated in black and white art deco, sprawling, quiet as the museum after hours.

"Mrs. Knowles called to say I should let you in and then to leave immediately for health reasons." Betty already had her coat on. "Should I stay, or will you lock up when you finish?"

"I'll take care of it. Thank you," Athena smiled up at Betty, who almost ran out the door and slammed it shut behind her.

"I've been here many times for parties. The master bedroom is this way." She led Drew through the large white and gold bedroom into Penelope's enviably spacious dressing room and closet.

On a large brass hook next to the three-way mirror hung a pale yellow velvet gown with a natural-size design of tulips and leaves in yellow satin and trimmed with white satin bows tipped with rhinestone ornaments.

I never examined this Worth evening gown.

Disappointment rooted her to the thick, plush white carpet. "Oh, no! It's not one of the two gowns I actually touched before I became ill."

Drew moved past her to the dress. "That must mean all four Bertha Palmer gowns are infected. We need to take this one back to the lab." He reached out.

"Don't touch it!" She grabbed his hand away just as his fingers brushed the delicate velvet.

He glanced over his shoulder at her. "This is Clayworth property. Clayworth responsibility."

"This isn't all about you," she declared, stepping between him and Bertha's infected gown. "It's about preserving pieces of Chicago's heritage. Children need a sense of history. If we all studied the past, we wouldn't keep making the same stupid mistakes. Stand over there and let me handle this."

She ignored him to slip on Playtex gloves and shake out a long, heavy plastic bag from her black tote.

With exaggerated care, she adjusted the dress on the gold padded hanger and slowly zipped the bag. "There. Safe."

"All right. Now we take it to Lewis Stemmer's lab," Drew said matter-of-factly like the decision had been made.

A vise squeezed Athena's chest, like one of Bertha's corsets. The gown looked forlorn in its clear, sterile bag. It was to be treated with the respect its workmanship deserved.

"Oh, no, we don't. The museum has the best resources for the gown—it needs to go into a proper cold-storage unit."

He narrowed his eyes, so she couldn't read them. "I've let you do this much. No more. You could become ill again."

She thrust her chin toward the ten-foot ceiling. "I'll risk it to save this dress."

His mouth set in a long line. "I'm not willing to let you risk it."

His arrogance made her even more determined. "Well, you'll just have to get used to it if you want my help to find the rest of the dresses. We're going to *my* lab whether you like it or not."

When Drew followed Athena into the pristine lab in the bowels of the museum, the same young girl who had been at the hospital gave him a long look.

Do I look as agitated as I feel? This is too risky for Athena, and she damn well knows it.

He rolled his shoulders, stress making him hot under the collar.

"Makayla, we've found one of Bertha's dresses. I'm sorry, but I must ask you to leave now. I don't want to risk you getting infected." Athena held open the door.

Makayla had one of those faces that's easy to read. Disappointment was written all over it.

"Why can't I stay? I'm willing to risk it, and think about how educational it will be for me to watch you at work on this. It may be an awesome, once-in-a-lifetime opportunity for me. It kinda makes up for my not being able to go out to the Secret Closet with you."

He tried to read Athena's eyes but couldn't because of those damn tinted lens. But her lips curved in the familiar way he remembered. Loving. Like she looked at her sisters.

And at me a lifetime ago.

"You're right, Makayla." Athena shut the door and swept up gloves, lab coat, and mask. "But full gear. And you sit over there on the stool. Away from the dress. No arguments. You, too," she muttered, thrusting a mask and gloves at Drew before putting on her own.

He watched her slowly ease the dress out of the bag

and hang it next to a table holding a long white box. "I'll get the sample for Dr. Stemmer."

Drew hovered at her back while she scraped minute particles from the dress fabric into a vial. He'd swear she held her breath until she finished and stepped away.

"All right," she breathed. "I remember now what happened with the Dior dress that infected my friend T. A. Long. The warm climate in the vault speeded up the breakdown of the boning in Bertha's dresses. The chemicals in the boning started to act up, and nasty bits pushed to the surface and came into contact with my skin. It became airborne, like a gas, which is what I also breathed in. Obviously, the same thing happened to Penelope."

Enthralled by her intensity and her long, delicate fingers, he couldn't take his eyes off her as she slowly, almost sensually, arranged the dress in the white casket-like box, loosely wrapping it in a length of unbleached muslin.

She looked up and appeared startled, like she'd forgotten everyone else in the room. "Come with me so you can give a full report to Dr. Stemmer."

He followed her to a huge walk-in refrigeration unit, where she placed the long casket on a metal shelf.

"By placing the gown in cold storage, the degradation process is slowed down significantly. This unit is fitted with vents to filter any nasty airborne toxins." She shut the refrigerator door and sighed. "Don't worry, I'll monitor it carefully."

He didn't miss the thread of stress in her voice or the way her fine-boned shoulders slumped.

She needs a backrub. Like I gave her on the beach when her broken ankle ached. Her skin felt like silk.

"You need a backrub to relax." His words stunned him. He'd been thinking them, and they came out.

Athena's head snapped up and she looked at him, glanced at the refrigerator door and back at his face.

"Drew, how do you feel? Dizzy? A headache? Are you seeing things?"

Yeah, he *saw* Athena, from her golden hair to her dainty feet. The embodiment of every adolescent boy's dream of a goddess, like her namesake, the goddess Athena. She'd always been his.

No, she was mine when I was a stupid kid, not now.

"You're looking kinda weird, Mr. Clayworth. Would you like to sit down?" Makayla called from the stool.

Christ, he'd forgotten he and Athena weren't alone in the room. He couldn't seem to concentrate on anything except Athena and wishing she'd take off those damn glasses so he'd know what she felt right now, this minute, for him.

Did everyone else know she was hiding behind them?

Or only me, because I know her so well?

Knew her, he reminded himself.

Athena stared at him so long, his gut clenched. Had he said the words out loud? He shook his head to clear it. *Christ, I barely touched Bertha's dress.*

"Drew, we need to take you to the hospital," she said softly with a note of real concern in her voice that could melt an iceberg.

But not me.

He backed up two steps, putting some space between them. He needed to get out of here before he said or did something he'd regret.

"No. I'm fine. I'm going home to sleep it off."

CHAPTER 8

Athena couldn't sleep off her guilt.

She rose at dawn to pace in front of her fireplace. She shouldn't have let Drew leave on his own. He *had* looked flushed, and his eyes had blazed even bluer, if possible. She should have gone after him.

She glanced at the mantel clock. In three hours she needed to be at Pandora's Box to price gowns she'd bought at an estate weeks ago.

Before I go, I'll just try to call him once. Only once, to make sure he's all right.

Drew didn't answer at his office at Clayworth's the second time, or the third, or on his cell, so she did the only sensible thing she could under the circumstances.

Bridget, head of security for John Clayworth and Company, answered on the first ring.

"Drew was in the store bright and early this mornin'. He told me the happy news about the dress."

Athena heard the relief in Bridget's voice.

"How did he look?" Athena asked as casually as she could muster.

"You know, now that you mention it, he did look flushed. But he must feel good. Told me he was goin' sailin' on the Skokie Lagoons off Tower Road like he usually does this time of year."

"Thanks, Bridget. I'll talk to him later."

Really, she *should* be talking to him about the next step in their hunt.

Her need to see him had everything to do with the dresses and nothing to do with wanting to find out if he'd been infected and could use her help.

She kept reminding herself of that fact as she walked slowly from the parking lot toward the Skokie Lagoons in Winnetka.

She'd just make sure he'd returned to his usual arrogant self, and then she'd be on her way to Pandora's Box, where she should be this very minute. And as soon as she finished there, she'd go to Lou Hinshaw's Auction House, the first on her list to check out for Bertha's gowns.

All at once she saw Drew leaning over what looked like a dingy with a sail. Muscles rippled under his blue polo shirt, and his suntanned arms flexed as he worked.

She stopped. *He's fine. I don't need to do this!*

She twirled to run away.

"Athena!" he shouted.

He's seen me. She had no choice but to twirl back and walk toward him.

She absolutely refused to be embarrassed while he eyed her huge tortoiseshell Tom Ford sunglasses she wore instead of her tinted ones, paused on the khaki shorts covering *just* enough of her thighs, and ended at her sensible rubber-soled shoes.

"You look like you weigh around a hundred and fifteen pounds. My Penguin sailboat requires no more than two hundred and ninety pounds of weight, which, if my calculations are correct, makes the two of us perfect."

He's hallucinating. Guilt ridden, she stepped closer. "Drew, you need to go home and rest."

He squinted his eyes against the bright sun. Now he looked more than ever like a young Paul Newman in *Cat on a Hot Tin Roof.*

But I'm definitely not Maggie, gazing at him with lust in my heart—or am I?

"Athena, my crewman can't make it today. I'm merely suggesting, since you're here, you help me out. Why are you here?"

Mortified to have been so worried when he couldn't have looked healthier, she lifted her chin to the sky. "I'm here to find you so we can scour the city for Bertha's dresses. Time is running out." She had less than two weeks.

Rebecca's cameraman had caught *this* smile on film. His *real* smile, which she'd first glimpsed in her seventeenth summer.

"I promise we'll leave no stone unturned to find those dresses. After we sail. Deal, partner?"

It seemed childish to refuse him. And really, he did look the tiniest bit flushed.

Maybe I should watch him for a little while longer.

"Oh, all right. Since I'm here. Now what?"

"You sit in the bow." He cast her a side glance.

"Remember the bow is the front and the stern is the back, where I steer."

"Of course I know the bow from the stern," she insisted indignantly. *I just can't ever remember which side is starboard and which is port.*

Hoping she wouldn't need to know, she studied the tiny spot he indicated in the point of the bow. "I can't fit one thigh in there!"

His gaze lingered on both her thighs. "Sure you can. Let me help you." He held her hand and maneuvered her around the wooden centerboard to settle in her spot with a little room to spare. She felt warm and loosened the top button of her blouse.

Overhead, the small white sail stretched to catch the wind.

She became aware of the soothing, quiet noise of water sloshing against the bow and of the sunlight turning Drew's fair hair every color from citron to amber.

The sound of the water and the breeze gently playing across her bare skin made her drowsy. The tight, warm tension in her chest eased, and she took a deep breath of fresh, green-scented late-spring air.

"I can't take the boat directly into the wind," Drew called out to her. "We'll tack to port. Tack to starboard. Keep an even keel to get where we want to go. Relax and we'll do this together."

It all came back to her, helping him race his small sailboat along the beach at the Clayworth Compound. She shifted to one side and then the other for balance, to help make the boat go faster. She tried to move carefully, but every single part of this boat seemed to be sharp, jutting, or just plain hard. *I'm definitely out of practice.*

She couldn't escape getting bumped and bruised. She did all she could to dodge the bits of the boat as they came at her.

After a while the rhythm came back to her. Like in the old days when the world distilled down to the power of the boat beneath her racing the waves and the awe of watching Drew capture the wind and make it do what he wanted.

Here, for one bright, shining moment like in *Camelot,* the world became crystal clear. Like it had been when they were kids.

Flying spray against her warm cheek broke the spell. For a few precious minutes she *had* let go of duty, regret, and sorrow. But they weren't kids anymore, setting sail for endless horizons. All their choices, plus her dad, were in this boat with them. Despite all their baggage, she couldn't deny the little flutters of excitement at being here with Drew again.

She watched him jump to shore and pull the boat higher onto the bank. She climbed out before he could help her and peered up at him. "Now can we get back to sleuthing?"

He nodded. "It felt good, though, didn't it?"

His gaze made her feel like the sun concentrated all its beams directly on her, and its powerful heat made it hard to breathe. She raised her hand to push back her hair, heavy and hot on her neck, and his gaze fell on the inside of her right wrist.

"Christ, you got that sailing with me." He lifted her arm where a small bright purple bruise had formed, gently sliding his fingers over the aching spot.

Shivers, like the waves against the bank at her feet, washed over her hot, tingly skin.

"Sorry about this." Abruptly, he dropped her arm.

Relieved, she stepped back. She shouldn't have worried. He appeared totally fine. Totally coherent. Totally in control, like all Clayworths.

He stepped back further. "Thanks for coming. I'll be in touch."

The real reason she'd come, the reason she'd never before admitted to herself, settled like an anchor in a region near her heart.

I came because I need closure with you. And I didn't know it until I inhaled truth serum. Now what should I do to fix it?

By Monday, Athena needed to fix her body. Every muscle felt stiff from stretching, or sitting on that hard, two-inch piece of wood, or whatever she'd done to herself while sailing. Bruises in colors ranging from dirty orange to bright purple were arranged in clusters like the constellations on one shoulder and thigh.

Obviously, she'd become so rusty at sailing it might be right up there with singing on the list of her un-accomplishments.

To stop thinking about sailing with *him,* and to deal with her disappointment about her stop at Hinshaw's Auction House, which came up with zero, and to keep herself busy while waiting for her appointments with four other dealers, Athena roamed around the large collection-storage room optimistically choosing more pieces for the Founding Families Exhibit, which might never happen.

Makayla walked in and immediately spied the bruise on Athena's wrist. "What happened to you?"

"I went sailing with Drew Clayworth. This is nothing. *This* is the really big one. I think it looks like Orion, don't you?" she asked Makayla, who peered at her shoulder.

A frown curved Makayla's pale lips, and the tiny diamond piercing her right eyebrow seemed to wink at Athena in alarm.

Not wanting to worry her, Athena laughed and pulled her blouse back up on her shoulder. "I'm fine. I actually had fun. I'd forgotten how much I love the feel of racing the wind. Drew does it really well."

"I've never heard you sound so, kind of, breathless." Makayla did a mock swoon. "Here I thought all the Clayworth men were, like, a necessary evil. Like money bags for the museum."

"Makayla, we never refer to our biggest donors, the Clayworths, as money bags," Athena gently reminded her.

"I watched *Talk of the Town* at the group home. That shot of you and Mr. Clayworth standing with Junior between you had like an awesome vibe. The other girls at the house asked if the two of you were like a really hot item."

Stunned by the question, Athena looked up from removing a Charles James dress from its double casket to find Makayla staring at her, a rapt expression on her face.

"Absolutely not." Technically, she wasn't lying. When Drew stroked her arm, she'd felt more alive than she had in years, but she couldn't read anything deeper on his charming exterior.

"You knew him before, right? Like your families were friends?"

"A long time ago." Athena nodded, trying to figure out how to be as truthful as possible with Makayla.

"You guys were never into each other, huh?"

Athena looked away, *refusing* to let the memories of their last night on the Clayworth terrace back in. "Something like that."

Makayla groaned. "Bummer! You were and he wasn't, right?"

Athena stared up into Makayla's intent face and put on her older-sister hat. "You might say we weren't on the same page at the same time. It happens that way sometimes, and then you get over it and move on," she said in what she hoped sounded like a positive, mature tone.

"Sometimes. Like on Rebecca's show and again in the lab that night I saw something sad on your face. Like maybe you're not over it? Would you tell me if I'm right?"

Am I having another bout of truthfulness from Bertha's stays?

No, she simply couldn't lie to this young girl, so alone in the world, who trusted her.

"He was my best friend, and I blew it," Athena admitted for the first time in her life.

"He was your BFF and he dumped you! Did you make him pay?" Makayla asked, indignation firing in her eyes. "You should have done it even if he's always been this rich, powerful dude. There's still time. We could make him fall in love with you, and then you could dump him this time."

Confronted by Makayla's teenage vengeance, Athena felt as ancient as Greek mythology. "It was a long time ago. He was only nineteen. He'd just lost his parents in a horrible sailboat accident. I couldn't do anything to hurt him."

But I did.

Makayla nodded. "You and your sisters always like to fix stuff. Like three fairy god-sisters. It's awesome. Everybody knows about it. Leonard and I talk about it all the time. Rebecca Covington-Sumner even wrote about it in her column once. Did you want me as an intern because I lost my mom and dad, too? Did you want to fix things for me because you couldn't fix Mr. Clayworth?"

The rush of sympathy, of memories of Drew as a wounded teenager, had consumed Athena as she'd read Makayla's application and looked into her soulful eyes. Very different eyes than Drew's. Not startling blue, glistening with unshed tears that had ripped her heart out. But lost, like he'd looked.

Yes. But I didn't realize it until this instant.

Athena smiled, fighting back tears and regrets and a million other feelings welling up from where she'd buried them so long ago. "You earned this internship because you're wonderful and brilliant." *And I want you to stay this way and not change like Drew did.*

Dazed by this newest epiphany, Athena gave Makayla a huge hug. "Now be your wonderful, brilliant self and finish cataloguing these pieces for me while I go to my last hopes of where a fence might have tried to sell Bertha's gowns in the city."

The House of Flan looked pained at the very idea they would buy from a fence.

Southley's practically showed Athena the door.

Kristie's *did* tell her they were insulted they were even on her list of establishments that would be approached with stolen property and *did* show her the door. Ever so politely, of course.

By the time Athena walked into Lance Simmons Antiques, her hopes of finding a lead to the dresses were pretty much gone. She could barely muster a smile for Viola Bloom, Lance's assistant, who stood at the reception desk waiting for her.

"I'm sorry, Athena, but Lance wants me in his office for an important meeting. I'm sure I'll only be a few minutes."

Nodding, Athena flung herself into a chair to wait.

Little screams of pleasure coming from Lance's office drove her to the open door.

Viola clung to Lance, sobbing all over his cream-on-cream striped silk three-piece suit. Over his shoulder, she looked up at Athena. "We're getting married!" she cried and thrust out her hand to reveal a magnificent square-cut emerald ring worth a fortune.

"I must call my mother," Viola gasped, then threw Lance a kiss and rushed past Athena, who stood in the doorway.

Lance sat down hard on the cream leather couch, where he blended right in except for his flushed cheeks and red mutton-chop sideburns.

Athena didn't need to see his slightly unfocused watery-brown eyes to realize Bertha's degrading stays had struck again.

"Lance, you need to see your doctor," Athena said gently and perched beside him.

"I've never felt better in my life," he boomed, beating

his chest with his fists. "I'm sweeping the woman of my dreams off her feet. We're leaving all of this behind." He gestured to his office full of beautiful antiques. He squinted at his snuffbox collection displayed prominently on the cherry bookcase. "Not all," he amended. "We're taking our favorites to fill the bed and breakfast we'll purchase in Sonoma Valley. With a vineyard. We'll have our own label. Called Viola," he sighed.

Honestly, Athena had never seen him look so blissful, even when acquiring a priceless artifact for a pittance. She wanted to be gentle. "Lance, I wish you both so much happiness, but—"

"No more buts! No more doubts. Now the world is clear, like the finest piece of crystal," he interrupted, surging to his feet. "I thought perhaps Viola has been my devoted assistant for thirty years because I paid well. I thought perhaps she doesn't feel the same way about me that I feel for her. But now I know all of that to be false." He sighed, and a deep crease appeared between his bushy red eyebrows. "Maybe all this time I should have been asking if the items I've been purchasing were hot, instead of keeping my mouth shut and doing the deal under the table."

All at once he beamed up at her, looking positively angelic. "But maybe now I will, because I'm a manly man again!"

"I can see that." Athena stood eyeball to eyeball with him. "About those items you should have inquired about. The last one was a Bertha Palmer gown, right?"

He stared at her. "Why, yes. Glorious piece. Exquisite workmanship. I handled it myself. I sold it to one of my best clients, Shelby Anderson, a few hours ago. She fell in love with it."

Athena held his eyes in a steely stare. "Lance, this is very, very important. I need her address and phone number at once."

His posture screamed indignation. "You know very well Viola and I never divulge details of our client list. We are sworn to secrecy. Never, I say! Never will I tell you she lives in Lincoln Park. I say, is it hot in here?" Lance asked, running one finger around his tight shirt collar.

"Yes. Sit down." She wanted to keep prodding him for the address, but he needed help, and she had another idea. "I'll send Viola in to you, and she'll take you someplace where you'll feel much better very soon."

"Thank you, dear Athena," he smiled up at her. "Be blissful, my dear, and make the right choices."

"I'm working on it." She blew him a kiss and went to find Viola weeping into the phone.

Athena touched her shoulder. "You need to take Lance to the Northwestern ER. Ask for Dr. Lewis Stemmer."

Viola dropped the receiver and curled both hands around her ring. "Is he all right? He isn't having second thoughts about us, is he?"

"No, he'll remember that he loves you. Everything will be fine. When you reach the ER, Dr. Stemmer will explain what is happening."

Love appeared to be the constant with the truth serum. Oh, yes, Athena had had her moment of clarity, but it had confused her even more.

She remembered loving Drew so much she ached with it. But it had been a mistake then. And now. Drew had never forgiven her for her second mistake with him.

She didn't want to make any new mistakes in their hunt for Bertha's gowns.

She knew there were probably dozens of Andersons living in Lincoln Park, but most of them no doubt had one thing in common besides their name. She headed straight to Clayworth's.

Drew sat in his office listening to Connor report that so far Ed had come up empty-handed in his investigation. Drew hoped Athena could come up with more. Time was running out. He was leaving for the Fastnet in two weeks and they had to find the dresses before then.

A sound in the doorway made him glance up.

For a heartbeat he thought he might be hallucinating, because he *wanted* to see her. Like last night he'd muttered everything he'd wanted to say.

He pulled himself together and stood up. "Perfect timing, Athena. We were talking about the investigation."

"I have a lead on another dress."

Connor shot her a hard look. "Where did you get your information?"

Athena shook her head and moved close enough so Drew could see the small bruise on her wrist.

"It doesn't matter. I believe it was bought in good faith by a Shelby Anderson."

"Christ, Athena," Drew laughed. "There are thousands of Andersons in the greater Chicago area."

Her smile lit up the room. "I know, but this one lives in Lincoln Park, and what do you bet she has a Clayworth charge card like most women in the city? If there's more than one Shelby Anderson, we'll check them all until we find the right one."

That edge of desire and delight he'd felt in the lab came roaring back. This time he knew it couldn't be exposure to truth gas. He remembered it from other times and places as pure Athena.

"Brilliant. Check on it, Connor."

"It's against Clayworth policy to give out information about our customers."

Connor's standard reply didn't surprise him.

Drew tried to meet Athena's eyes, or as much of them as he could see through those damn glasses. "There's a first time for everything."

Her face flushed. "Thank you."

"Don't thank me. I think it's a mistake." Connor shot them both hard looks and walked out.

Athena slid down into the heavy black stuffed leather chair in front of his desk.

Drew came around toward her. "You look tired."

She laughed. "Just what a girl likes to hear. So much for Clayworth charm."

Amused, he leaned on the desk in front of her. "Can I get you anything?"

"More time. It's running out."

"I know." It suddenly hit him like a blow to the chest. Because of the crisis with Athena and the dresses, he might not sail in the Fastnet. The thought drove him back behind the desk that had been his father's and grandfather's and the founder's, John Clayworth. Years of tradition. A name to protect at all costs.

"Sorry, but you do look tired. Rest. I'll go see what Connor has dug up."

From the doorway he heard her deep sigh and stared back at her. Her hair spilled over the back of the chair where she rested her head on the soft leather.

Instead of going straight into Connor's office next

door, he stopped in the butler's pantry between the two rooms. A decade ago there had been a butler and a formal dining room, which now served as the boardroom. They all fended for themselves these days.

Connor found him staring into the refrigerator.

"We'll have an answer in the next twenty minutes. What are you doing?"

Drew pulled out a bottle of sparkling water and a bottle of Duval-Leroy champagne. "Deciding which I should take to Athena. She looks like she could use a drink."

"Don't let her hurt you again."

His words hit Drew like an icy wave, cooling the hot excitement he'd felt since Athena walked into the room. Keeping his face unreadable, Drew turned to Connor, the brother he'd never had. The only person who knew how much Athena had hurt him when he was so raw with pain. "It was a long time ago."

Connor pushed his fingers through his unruly dark hair in the gesture that told everyone he felt embarrassed to be getting too personal, butting in where he shouldn't. Drew wasn't the only Clayworth to keep his emotions private. They each handled it in different ways.

"I know you cared about her once."

Drew shrugged. "Don't worry. I'm immune now."

"I hope so, because with her dad's trouble, nothing good could come out of you getting involved again. If you want to talk about it, I'm here."

For Connor, this exchange took real caring and commitment, and Drew didn't make light of it. He didn't want to talk about his feelings for Athena. Christ, he didn't ever want to *feel* anything for her, but he did.

He put the bottles down on the polished marble

counter and clasped Connor's shoulder. "I promise I'll work this mess out with Athena to protect myself and Clayworth's."

Athena heard Connor's voice and Drew's coming through the small door in the middle of the wall of bookcases. Thinking it might be news, she went to find out.

They were standing in a long, narrow butler's pantry, lined with cabinets of rare Circassian walnut and black marble.

"Did you find Shelby Anderson?"

They both looked up. Connor blushed to the roots of his dark hair, and Drew gave her his most insincere smile.

"We should have it by now. I'll be back." Connor bolted from the room, leaving Athena to wonder what she'd interrupted.

"Champagne or sparkling water?" Drew asked smoothly, holding up frosty bottles of both.

"Nothing, thank you. Has something happened?" she asked, sensing a new tenseness in him. A few minutes ago he'd seemed easier, approachable. Lance had urged her to make wise choices. She had to pick the right moment to put her past with Drew out on the table and talk about it from the perspective of two mature adults, not the children they'd been. He'd been right to say she looked tired. Tired of unhappiness and confusion. More than time to have this out with him.

"Drew, has something happened?" she asked again.

"Nothing's changed. Trouble is trouble." His face unreadable, he placed the bottles back in the refrigerator.

Connor came in and handed a sheet of paper to Drew.

"There are three Shelby Andersons in Lincoln Park. One on Armitage. One on Fullerton, and one on Dickerson. But we have no proof that any of these are who you are looking for. Why would the thieves fence the gowns so quickly and so close to home?"

Excitement burned away Athena's fatigue. "For a lawyer, you know precious little about the criminal mind. The gowns are hot. They want to unload them before they get caught. Bertha Palmer is a legend in Chicago, and all the best collectors are here. Give me the addresses so we can go and find out right now."

Drew stared at her. "What are you suggesting? That we don't call them first?"

"And say what? Hi, did you recently purchase a hot Bertha Palmer gown? Oh, and by the way, it's infected with a truth serum, so please beware." She thrust her chin up, determined to make this happen now. "I'm suggesting we go to these addresses to help Shelby and retrieve the gown. If they aren't the *right* Shelby Anderson, we'll be like that couple on television who goes around giving unsuspecting people a million dollars. Except it will be a shopping spree at Clayworth's given out by the CEO himself."

Connor shook his head. "As your lawyer, the less I know of this, the better. I'll alert Lewis we might have a lead. Drew, watch yourself and call me if you need me. I'll be ready."

For some odd reason, Connor threw her a narrow, hard look of anger before he turned on his heels and left them alone.

Warmth coursed through her veins. A tiny gleam of delight gleamed in Drew's eyes. "Connor's right. This is crazy, but so is the whole situation. Let's go, partner, and get this over with."

Yes, if she ever hoped to get over Drew she needed to confront him openly.

And she would. As soon as they saved Shelby Anderson and Bertha's gown.

CHAPTER 9

Athena and Drew agreed to start on Fullerton and work their way deeper into Lincoln Park.

The first Shelby Anderson's ultramodern condo overlooked Lincoln Park Zoo, which seemed to delight her triplet four-year-old daughters who were giggling at the large windows. *This* Shelby had never heard of Bertha Palmer. Only the Palmer House Hotel, where they'd stayed for a week when the family moved to Chicago from Dubuque, Iowa.

Athena believed her.

The Shelby on Armitage turned out to be a guy who was drinking beer with his buddies while they watched the Cubs game on television. He insisted on knowing what he'd won at Clayworth's, because his fiancée ran his card to the max every month. Without hesitation, Drew gave his private number and told him to call for his prize.

As they walked toward Dickerson, Athena slid Drew

a sheepish look. "Sorry. This was all my idea. What are you giving him?"

"A zero balance on his Clayworth charge card."

A warm, fuzzy feeling tingling to her toes, she grinned. "That's very generous, Drew."

He laughed. "No. It's expedient."

The instant Athena looked up at the imposing Victorian mansion in the heart of Lincoln Park, she sensed they'd come to the right place at last.

"This is it. Someone who lives in a house like this would love Bertha," she told Drew and sprinted up the tall front steps. She pressed the brass doorbell just as Drew came up beside her.

"Hi, y'all, who's there?" came a light, feminine voice from the intercom system embedded in the thick, wide doorframe.

"Shelby, it's Drew Clayworth from John Clayworth and Company."

He couldn't have sounded more warm and inviting. She actually felt a bit warm herself, but she put it down to excitement.

"Sugar, I love your store. Come on in. The door's open."

Drew met her eyes. "You're right. I believe we have a live one. I'm calling Connor for backup."

Too anxious to wait, Athena pushed the door open.

They entered a long, narrow wood-paneled foyer vibrating with the blare of a television or radio. It became louder and more distinct the deeper they walked down a hall lined with rare old botanical prints she'd seen months ago at Lance's antique house.

They stepped into a sunny kitchen and family room

with a huge flatscreen television tuned to the Paula Deen show on the Food Network.

A tall, incredibly thin woman, wearing Bertha's yellow satin Worth gown, looked up at them. Athena's stomach turned over at the sight of the skirt, bordered with puffings of two shades of yellow chiffon and velvet, dragging on the quarry tile floor.

"Stay here," Drew ordered in his old authoritarian voice, not his signature charming banter.

It took all Athena's willpower to let him take the lead and not rush to pick up the hem of the dress.

The dress sleeves, designed to make Bertha's arms appear like stems coming out of gold silk velvet flowers, slid off Shelby's narrow shoulders as she twirled away from the stove and toward them. Her green eyes looked huge in her small face. "Paula says get your butter on!"

Instinctively, Athena stepped forward to throw herself between the dress bodice, embroidered with silver cord, gold beads, sequins, and rhinestones, and the butter spitting out of the skillet.

Drew stepped in front of her and refused to move. Even going so far as to hold her behind his back in an iron grip.

"Let me go," she grunted.

"Behave for a change. Remember this isn't about us," he muttered, making so much sense she shut up.

"Shelby, I'm Drew Clayworth. I've come to help you."

Shelby threw back her head and laughed with amazing gusto for someone who looked so fragile.

"Honey pie, if you want to help, grab a stick of butter—we're doin' it southern style!"

She twirled back to the stove and threw two more

sticks of butter into the hot, sizzling frying pan. Drew reached out to take her arm, but Shelby swished toward the refrigerator before he could stop her.

She pulled out what looked like a key lime pie and seemed to be looking *past* them to something beyond. "I cooked my Stevie's favorite. Where is my Stevie?"

Drew bore down on Shelby, Athena right behind him, stopping only long enough to turn off the flame under the sizzling skillet.

"Shelby, let me help you."

"If you help, you can have a helpin', honey pie. I'm from Georgia. We know how to be hospitable." She danced toward the table and stumbled on the double lace ruffle of the underskirt.

Athena stifled a gasp as Drew grabbed Shelby's thin upper arm. "Let's sit down first." He helped her onto the bleached oak dining chair, never taking his eyes off her. "This pie looks delicious. We'll put it back into the refrigerator for now. Steve will be here soon."

Shelby nodded. "My Stevie is the most gentle, tender, and sweet man ever." She stuck three fingers into the pie and came out with a big glob of filling and whipped cream. "As sweet as this here pie," she muttered, licking her fingers.

Panting, a tall man, striped tie askew, raced into the kitchen.

"Thank God she's all right," he gasped, staring at his wife sticking her fingers into the pie for the second time.

Shelby appeared oblivious to everything except repeatedly plunging her fingers into the pie, lifting out bigger globs, and sticking all of them in her mouth at the same time.

Drew stayed by her side and beckoned Steve closer. "You received a call from Clayworth's and Dr. Lewis Stemmer?"

Steve nodded, staring at his wife in obvious concern. "Yes. They told me an ambulance is on the way and the effects of the toxins should wear off by morning."

In the distance Athena heard the thin wail of a siren.

Shelby's head snapped up. A mustache of key lime lined her upper lip. "Hi, Stevie. You know how you're always tellin' me I should eat more. This afternoon I put on this pretty dress and I had a vision as clear as a bell ringin' on Sunday morning. You're right, and I haven't been cookin' enough, either. I'm a darn fine cook, and I love healthy good food. Silly of me to choose not to do somethin' I love. I'm going to write a cookbook with my great-great-great grandma Shelby's recipes." She fanned herself with both hands. "I must have left the oven on. It's mighty hot in here."

"Sugar, you're going to the hospital, where it will be cooler," Steve said softly.

Drew helped her to her feet. "Shelby, I promise you'll feel better there."

A little ache had started in Athena's stomach the instant she saw how gently and kindly Drew helped Shelby. No charming handsome mask, but real emotion on his face. *This* man deserved to be obeyed, so she did what he'd asked and stayed out of harm's way.

Steve hovered on one side of Shelby, and Drew supported her on the other.

As they moved toward the hall, Athena stepped back.

Shelby looked her straight in the eyes. "Hi there. Do you like my dress?"

Stunned, Athena blurted out the truth. “I love it. I’d like to have it.”

“I knew another gal would appreciate how pretty it is.” She sent a coy, unfocused glance between the two men holding her up. “It’s like the one my great-great-great grandma Shelby wore to her cotillion in Atlanta. There’s a paintin’ of it in my aunt Scarlett’s house on Peachtree. It’s the reason I bought this dress from the dealer.” She giggled and leaned closer. “I think it might be hot, ’cause it sorta looks like a picture I saw of Bertha Palmer at the museum. Don’t tell Lance,” she whispered.

Athena met Drew’s eyes, and a silken fiber of old yearnings pulled her to him. Athena smiled. “I promise I won’t tell, Shelby.”

Athena followed them out onto the porch, then down the stairs, and stood beside the ambulance while the paramedics helped Shelby inside.

Drew looked up at the paramedic coming back out. “Miss Smith is an expert on how to stabilize the toxin. Did Dr. Stemmer send the materials for her to contain the dress?”

The paramedic nodded and thrust the package containing masks, gloves, and plastic at her.

“Steve, we need to get that infected dress off of Shelby. Then you can ride to the hospital with her,” Drew ordered.

Shaken by his tenderness with Shelby and more confused by him than ever, she took Drew’s hand to be helped into the ambulance. Her foot slipped off the low step, and he grabbed her to keep her from falling, holding her so tight she could feel his heart beating against her breasts.

Blood rushed to her head, a sudden disorientation, and the sound of her pounding pulse drowned out everything else.

I'm not immune at all.

She pulled free, and he helped her up into the low, cramped ambulance.

How stupid and juvenile to feel so hot and bothered, but she did, and she'd just have to deal with it. Or think about it tomorrow, like one of Shelby's southern belles. Now she needed to help Shelby out of this dress.

Her eyes closed, Shelby rested on the stretcher, one of her shoes hanging off her toes.

Athena carefully removed both shoes and laid a blanket over her.

Shelby giggled and wiggled while the paramedic checked her vitals and put in an IV line.

"We need to get you out of this dress, Shelby. I'm sorry if these rubber gloves feel cold." Athena slowly pulled the dress down Shelby's thin body and out from beneath the blanket.

"I'm glad I always followed my mama's orders never to leave the house without my good underwear on in case I was in an accident. From now on I'm only making good choices like that one," Shelby sighed.

Athena tucked the blanket around her neck. "Sleep now. I promise you'll feel better when you wake up."

We've all been the same way. Acting out our inner secret desires.

She contained the dress in plastic, all the while feeling Drew watching her through the open ambulance door. Had he felt anything when they touched for the first time when totally not under the influence? It had been so long.

She'd been seventeen and truly believed the Fates sent her out to the Clayworth patio to comfort him because only she could help him.

The love of my life, and I was the only one who could protect and love him the way he deserved.

She closed her eyes, saw herself kneel before Drew, look up into his face, felt his arms sweep her up in an embrace that had taken her breath away.

She sucked in a deep gulp of air and opened her eyes.

Here they were, thrown together again by another embarrassing moment, and she couldn't stop thinking about what might have been. She should be thinking about her sisters, and about her father at the small family compound in Palm Beach. She should be trying to understand what happened between the Clayworths and her father. She should be consumed by their search for the last two dresses.

She *was* consumed by her need to fix the past so she could move forward and honor her mother's memory with the scholarship fund.

Clutching the dress to her chest, she allowed both Steve and Drew to help her out of the ambulance.

Steve jumped inside to be with Shelby, and, sirens wailing, the ambulance roared off to the emergency room at Northwestern Hospital.

For a second she thought Drew would follow and something terribly important would be out of her reach. Then he turned.

He sighed and flexed his shoulders. "Later today when Shelby is feeling better, Connor will talk to her about the dress actually being Clayworth property. We're getting closer. I promise we'll find the last two stolen gowns."

No more mistakes. She knew what she needed to do. "When we do, will you keep your promise about allowing the museum to display them in our Founding Families Exhibit?"

His intent expression, searching her face, shook her resolve. Was he thinking about the promise she hadn't kept? "If I can," he finally uttered.

"Be at the museum at closing time tomorrow and I'll show you why you should."

She saw him stiffen as he studied her out of narrowed eyes. "Why?"

"I'm giving you a private tour of the existing exhibit. I want you to see why I need the dresses to expand it to what it should be."

He hesitated for two thuds of her heart against her ribs before he nodded.

"Great! See you tomorrow." She waved and swung away before he changed his mind.

At the museum, where she felt the most confident, she'd clear the air at last. Find some kind of closure with their past so she could stop thinking about what might have been and concentrate on what had to be done to keep her job and keep her promise to Makayla and her own family.

CHAPTER 10

Drew slowly climbed the curved staircase to the second floor of the Fashion Institute of Chicago.

He'd promised Connor he was immune to Athena. Impervious to old memories, old hurts. He'd meant it then. Now he wasn't so sure.

He'd come tonight to see Athena. See if she looked happier, like she had when they went sailing. Like she had yesterday when they found the second dress and stored it safely away. He'd come to make sense of their past.

On the steps of the ambulance, had she felt his rush of desire when, her breasts crushed to his chest, he'd held her too tight and too long? If she hadn't been wearing those damn glasses, he'd be able to see if it had affected her at all.

I won't let her break my heart again.

He stopped, wondering why in the hell he'd think such nonsense. Hearts didn't break. He knew about grief from personal experience. Knew losing a partner, parent, or child constituted the greatest stress the human psyche could ever suffer. He'd learned that, with time and help, people mended. Like he'd mended. Or he would finally mend, once he raced in the Fastnet for his parents.

At last the time had come. England. The Fastnet. His gut clenched with raw excitement. Only a few more details to work out. Decide among the different types of sea anchors to stop the boat's bow dead into the waves and the proper equipment to slow the boat when running before the wind. He'd been scheduled to look at some new technology tonight.

Instead he'd come here, because Athena asked and the promise he'd made himself had changed.

He stopped, realizing that again Athena had kept him from doing what needed to be done.

He shook off the feeling at the top of the staircase and turned left toward her office. Before he could knock, the door swung open.

Athena, still wearing those damn glasses, stood smiling up at him. "Welcome, Drew. I'm delighted to have this opportunity to show you what your generous support will do for the museum."

Her voice sounded different tonight. *Determined.* Curious, he peered past her, noticing picture frames scattered over a desk. The urge to get reacquainted, learn who she had become, got the best of him. "Let's start with your office." He strolled in, and she stepped back as if startled.

"Are you all right, Drew?" She shook her head, her light golden hair swinging against her neck. "No headache? No effects after being so close to Bertha's gown yesterday at Shelby's?"

He shrugged. "I'm good." He paced around, trying to rid himself of a sudden rush of adrenaline. The pictures on her desk were of her sisters, parents, and two cats. Obviously, Drusilla and Junior. He strolled past another neat desk and a small, well-organized table of files in the corner. He knew Athena would love the charm of the marble fireplace and had probably chosen the large red sofa in front of it. The room looked like her. Carried her light floral scent with a hint of spice. "Nice, big light room. As a trustee, I'm happy to see the museum provides a healthy work environment."

"Seen enough?" she asked, clearly confused.

Christ, I'm confused, too!

He needed more time. He looked around for an excuse to prolong this. "Hey, what's this?" He strolled over and opened a heavy carved door with a brass doorknob. The closet held nothing but one long black dress and a sachet of her perfume, more intense and exotic in the smaller space. "Roomy closet. Pretty dress. Yours?"

She stepped in front of him and closed the door. "I've seen your closet. It's much bigger than mine. Yes, thank you, it is my very special dress. My first vintage piece, which started my passion for all things old."

Does she have a passion for old relationships? I sure as hell do.

The idea smacked him in the face. Knocked all the other nonsense out of his head. He knew he'd come here tonight for this. To close the door on the past.

Or did I come to open a new one?

The need grew stronger watching Athena move with an unconscious grace across the room. He felt reckless, and the desire to see where this might lead drove him to smile and take her arm when she purposefully walked out into the hall. He felt her tense, but she didn't ask him to stop touching her. He didn't want to stop. They weren't teenagers any longer. He wasn't her hero, fallen off his pedestal, and she wasn't the perfect goddess he'd expected her to be.

"We're going to the Georgian Neoclassical room," she said quietly.

Still he held her arm, letting her lead him though the dimly lit museum. He knew from being a trustee that by this time the staff would be gone and the lone night guard made his rounds only every two hours.

Her heels clicked on the tile floor as she led him into the part of the museum full of arches and pillars. Even in the diffused light, the display cases of glassware and china gleamed in rich, vibrant colors along the circular walls.

She stopped in front of a long, low case. "This exhibit is the china and crystal that Chicago's founding families, the Palmers, Fields, and Clayworths, would have used for their lavish black tie dinner parties. These gold chargers and gold-rimmed crystal goblets are from your family."

He scrutinized the case, trying to appear interested. "Yeah. I remember these. We used them every night."

"You did not!" She laughed.

Captivated by the catch of happiness he heard in her voice for the first time, he grabbed her hand, rubbing his thumb lightly over the bruise at her wrist. "C'mon. Show me more."

Her blush made his blood pound.

He allowed her to slip out of his fingers, but he didn't take his eyes off her as she twirled around the room.

"For history to have social value, it needs to be personal and intimate, revealing the problems, the passions of people in the past. Then it connects with the present. Comes alive. I want you to imagine how this room will look when we get funding. This will be a ballroom. I want everyone to be able to see, *feel,* what it was like with music and beautiful people dancing. It's important to appreciate our rich history. It helps to better understand our more sterile world today. Perhaps encourage putting more beauty in our daily lives. Bertha's dresses will help make that happen."

The urge to do just that pulled him across the room to her side. "I'll make sure you get the dresses on two conditions."

She stared up at him. "There are no conditions. We have a deal."

God, I want to see your eyes. Need to know how you feel. Here. With me. Tonight.

He laughed, but the sound caught deep in his chest. "Humor me. Take off those glasses. They're always falling off your nose anyway." He slid them off her adorable nose before she could stop him.

"What are you doing? Give those back," she demanded, the words echoing against the high ceiling.

She cringed, looking guilty for not whispering in these hallowed halls.

Her eyes seemed bigger and a deeper aquamarine than they had in the hospital.

He held the glasses up and peered through them. Nothing but plain tinted glass. "You don't need these to see."

"What are you up to this time?" She glared and grabbed again for the glasses.

He jammed them into a front trouser pocket. "Come and get them," he dared.

He saw a nerve throbbing at her throat. His pulse seemed to be matching the beat.

She put her hands behind her back and glared at him.

"Hey, I'm performing a public service. On behalf of the museum, aren't you interested in my other condition?"

She thrust her chin to the ceiling. "I didn't ask you here to play games, Drew."

"You asked me here to prove your point. Fair enough." He rammed his hands into his pockets, fingering the delicate glass frames. "You get the Bertha gowns for your exhibit if you put on your black dress and help me *feel* a black tie affair here."

Her breasts beneath her white, silky blouse rose and fell. "Now *you're* hallucinating. I'm not putting my dress on for you."

Faking indifference, he shrugged. "As a contributor to the museum, all I'm asking is a sample of what the exhibit will look like. Your development department has done it many times before to solicit underwriting for exhibits. Think of it as your bit for historical preservation."

He saw faint amusement curve her full mouth, and her eyes widened like she'd thought of something exciting.

"All right. I'll do it. But it will cost you the dresses plus your help with Edna Keene and the board of trustees to gain support for the new scholarship program."

Exhilaration pumped through him. He sensed the dress had special meaning for her, and he wanted her to wear it for him. "Consider it done."

She shook her head, her hair looking like swirling

liquid gold around her shoulders. "This is utter madness. Wait here," she ordered. "I'll be back."

He watched her walk away. Halfway across the room, she stopped and looked back, like she'd felt him staring at her.

She flashed him a smile that had him drooling like those interns in the ER.

"Since we won't have any music for our ball, I'll sing."

"I *should* sing. That would teach him a lesson for blackmailing me into putting on this dress."

In the full-length mirror on the inside of the closet door, Athena watched herself fumble with the tiny buttons on the black gown. "No wonder Bertha needed two people to help her into dresses like this," she muttered to herself, finally managing to attach the last hook and eye.

Sucking in her stomach, she turned to view the dress. Thank God, it still fit her.

Her waist looked itsy-bitsy, her bosom full, her décolletage creamy against the jet and black velvet, her arms graceful in the long sleeves.

She stared at herself in the mirror. Maybe she didn't need the glasses. The haunted look in her eyes had faded. Now they looked wide and slightly wild.

"Because I'm scared half out of my wits. And obviously I've lost the other half of my mind, or I wouldn't be playing dress-up for Drew Clayworth. Dresses or no dresses." She laughed at her reflection. "It's official. I've totally lost my mind. I'm talking to myself."

She found the loop on the train, slid her finger into it, and lifted the hem. All right, she'd make him *feel* a black tie affair given in one of the great mansions on Prairie Avenue, old Chicago's "street of the stately few." His family had had a red-brick French-style mansion on the genteel, wealth-laden street back when Chicago's fans called the city the gem of the prairie and its critics called it a universal grog shop. Before all the oldest, wealthiest families moved to Lake Forest.

Inevitably, thoughts of the Clayworth estate brought visions of her and Drew on the fateful Christmas night. Tonight all the memories came out of hiding. *She* was coming out of hiding to close that door.

Terrified—but determined, she reminded herself—she glided back downstairs to explain her actions the night everything changed between them, and then she'd ask about her father. If her courage didn't fail her.

She found Drew leaning one broad shoulder against a pillar.

He lifted his eyebrows, straightened, and lazily strolled to where she waited in the center of the room.

"You look beautiful. I'm sorry I'm not wearing black tie."

"You're not sorry! I've seen the donor benefit guest list. You usually decline to put on your tux at the last minute."

"Guilty as charged." His beautiful mouth curled into a deep smile. He reached out and pulled her gently closer. "Shall we dance?"

A wicked little spark of excitement made her slowly smile back. "I'll hum."

"Go for it," he chuckled into her ear.

Held in his arms, gliding around the dim room, she began humming, "I Could Have Danced All Night."

It sounded truly awful, and she thought of stopping to put him out of his misery, but then she felt his slight wince and his arm tightened around her, trying to disguise his reaction.

Memories of other, happier times roared back. She hummed louder and broke into full song, sounding worse and worse.

She felt him shaking with silent laughter as he twirled her faster and faster around the dim room, the faint light a halo around them.

He chimed in with a nice clear tenor, as if trying to help her find the right key.

Refusing to give in, she sang even louder, her voice rising to a high, squeaky croak. He twirled her faster, their dreadful duet broken by snatches of their gasping laughter.

She tried to ignore the slow, warm, diffused excitement coming up from deep inside to glaze her skin with heat.

In the middle of the room, at the height of the song and their laughter, he dipped her so low her shoulder-length hair brushed the floor.

He brought her up, and his face looked alive with delight. "It's reassuring to mere mortals that you're not perfect. You still have a tin ear." He laughed like he couldn't stop. Deep, full of joy.

She caught it, joining in, dazzled by him.

He's close enough to kiss.

Her laughter died in her throat and she took one step back.

His arm tightened around her so she couldn't move.

Time fell away like it had in the Secret Closet. The past rushing forward to collide with the present.

He lifted her chin with his thumb, and she felt him stroke her cheek. Ever so slowly, he lowered his head and she closed her eyes, wanting his kiss.

His lips brushed against her mouth and a shock rippled through her body. For one insane instant, she opened her lips wider, letting his tongue trace the contours, tasting her. Tasting him. Molding her lips to his wonderful, warm, sensual mouth.

No!

Fear brought sanity, and she pulled away. She drew a deep, strengthening breath, trying to recapture her courage. "For a second you let me in," she whispered.

His eyes narrowed into slits, the concentrated cornflower blue seared through her. "I let you in once before. Remember?"

He opened the door, and she had to walk through.

"Yes, I remember. I betrayed you, and you'll never forgive me." She said it in all its stark reality.

Something flickered in his eyes. He dropped his arms and stepped back.

But he still seemed to be touching her. She felt his heat. Felt tension quivering around them. Time seemed to stand still. Waiting for her to make another mistake.

No matter what it cost her, she needed to finish what she'd started a lifetime ago. "I don't need your forgiveness for what I did. I'd like your understanding. I told your uncle that you were leaving school to go sail in the Fastnet because I was seventeen and terrified that you'd be killed like your parents. I truly believed that I was the only person on the planet who could keep you safe."

She forced herself to keep gazing into his eyes, to somehow penetrate the barriers he'd set up, so smooth, so light, so unassailable. "Maybe I could have done it differently, but I didn't know how. All I knew was that I had to risk losing our relationship to save you."

She had to look away, couldn't let him see what it cost her to dredge up these feelings of aching fear and love.

He gave nothing away. His face was cool and beautiful in the dim light.

I need to get away. Now!

She gathered up the hem of the gown in both fists. "I'll change and let you out. The security code is already set." She turned and ran.

She ran away from his silence The only answer he'd given. She knew it was stupid to go over the past like this, as if she could change it, or he could understand it at last.

How could she stop memories, really? They lived inside, replaying over and over the feeling of being kissed by Drew with a slow, sensual heat and wanting to kiss him back forever. Wanting to give him everything like she'd once offered. Like she'd offered tonight.

He'd rejected her then and now.

Drew let her go, determined to regain his usual detachment. Determined to stop his urge to go after her and pull her back into his arms.

Christ, he wanted to understand. Wanted to forgive. Wanted her.

Somewhere, back in the recesses of his subconscious, the truth knocked every other excuse over like a game of dominoes until any fool could see it. Without truth serum, with nothing but the ache in his gut, he knew he'd never stopped wanting her.

Just like he'd first wanted her at nineteen.

It had been inappropriate then. Absolutely. Impossible.

They had been too young, too inexperienced, and he had been too rubbed raw from pain.

Restless, he roamed around the room. All this sexual energy, all his aching regrets, all his pounding yearnings building inside him needed an outlet, a way to make her understand his feelings.

Christ, I need to understand.

He let all the memories roar back in. Athena breaking her promise to keep his secret. His rage and pain at being betrayed by the one person he trusted above all others. He'd been vulnerable on so many levels he couldn't admit. Sometimes he still felt like that vulnerable boy believing that he'd betrayed his parents with his judgment and they had betrayed him with their choice to leave him behind.

Then he'd been an impetuous kid, lashing out at the world, lashing out at Athena. Yes, she'd hurt him and potentially saved him by doing it. Or so she truly believed.

Maybe I believe her.

He stopped and gazed down at his family's trappings of wealth. The solid gold ornaments. The priceless jewels on the napkin holders. Beautiful, tangible symbols of their power. For one hundred and fifty years, Clayworths had taken chances, fought overwhelming odds to seize what they wanted.

He was a Clayworth to his very core, and he wanted Athena.

He slowly mounted the stairs.

CHAPTER 11

Athena's hand trembled so much she couldn't get proper hold of the tiny velvet buttons on the dress. She turned around, looked over her shoulder, and tried to see in the mirror why she couldn't get the darn thing open. If she weren't aquiver with remorse, embarrassment, and an odd, totally inappropriate excitement, she could get the job done.

I need to get the job done so I can get away from Drew.

Her upper right arm still ached from her efforts to help Drew sail. Straining with every ounce of dexterity she possessed, she managed to get the top three buttons loose.

"Only twenty more to go," she breathed, exhausted and so tense her body felt on fire. She knew she'd been right to confront him about the past, but she hadn't known how vulnerable it would make her feel to relive all the old, powerful emotions.

Closing her eyes, she took a deep breath for courage before opening them again.

In the mirror she saw Drew standing in the doorway.

She gasped and swung toward him, holding the dress to her heaving bosom. "I didn't hear you knock."

"I didn't knock." Their eyes locked as he clicked the door shut and walked toward her. "Do you need help?"

No, I'll call the security guard. No, I'll wear the dress home. No, I...

"Yes. The one other time I wore this dress, it wasn't as difficult." Then she remembered there'd been a saleswoman to help. She turned her back to him. "Please. I'm sorry. The buttons are really tiny."

"I have good hands."

His fingers were cool and gentle touching her back. She looked pointedly at the floor, trying to ignore her heart pounding against her ribs so hard she hoped he couldn't hear it.

Please, please don't let this be another mistake.

Mercifully, he had her unbuttoned in a few minutes. She looked up, just as one shoulder of the black dress slipped, exposing the bruise on her upper arm.

Their eyes met in the mirror when she tried to pull the dress back up.

His hand stopped her. "Did you get this sailing with me?"

Every instinct she possessed warned her to defuse this pulsing sensual tension between them. Tonight too much old emotion kept spewing out like an erupting volcano. Deep inside, she knew only more pain could come of this.

She forced a laugh, and it sounded pathetically fake in

her own ears. "Your sailing didn't give me these bruises. Your boat is the culprit. I think this one looks like a constellation. Quite poetic, since I earned it sailing and sailors once used the stars to navigate."

His fingers drifted over the bruise, and she shivered despite her best efforts not to respond.

"Ah, yes. This one definitely looks like Betelgeuse. It's a very prominent star; a right angle off the horizon at early dawn. One of my favorites."

He leaned down and pressed his lips to the aching bruise.

Pleasure melted her limbs, but she knew she needed to stop. She tilted her head back toward him. "Drew, we—"

His lips stopped her, kissing her. So hot, moist, sweet, and luscious, she felt all her good intentions dissolve away.

Little explosions went off in her head. In slow motion to draw out the pleasure, she turned so he could slide his hands inside the dress to span her naked waist with his fingers. He pulled her into him, and the dress slid down her arms.

He nuzzled her breasts, moving closer and closer to the sensitive, aching nipples, and she clung to him, barely able to stand.

The knock on the door struck like a lightning bolt, tearing them apart. Drew's eyes were a spectacle of light and blue like nothing she'd ever seen.

"Miss Smith, it's Leonard. Is everything all right?"

Clutching the dress bodice up across her scorching breasts, she trembled, hardly able to take in a breath for the ache in her chest.

She backed toward the door and caught one heel on the train, stumbling. Drew reached out to catch her.

Burning up with embarrassment, with regret, with a million reasons why this shouldn't have happened, she couldn't look at him. She opened the door just enough to peek around. Leonard's grizzled face appeared pinched with concern.

"Hi, Leonard. I'm working late. That's all." She forced her voice not to betray her breathless shaking.

"Needed to check. Saw your Jeep and Mr. Clayworth's silver Porsche in the executive parking lot."

"Yes. Mr. Clayworth is here discussing a new exhibit. He'll be leaving now. And I'll be going shortly."

"Fine." Leonard nodded. "Take your time. I'll be downstairs at the back entrance to let you both out."

She clicked the door shut and stood staring at it. Her grip on the dress cramped her fingers. "Please go, Drew," she whispered, ready to burst into loud, unattractive tears.

"Athena, look at me." He sounded like *her* Drew. Not the sweet, seductive voice he'd used tonight from the instant she opened the door to him. It brought back so many memories of their youth, when being with him, listening to him, made her believe the myths of undying love and heroes and Olympus-like passion were at her fingertips.

Pride and anger and the remnants of an unshakeable dignity handed down by her mother gave Athena the courage to turn and face him.

His eyes were larger, softer. "We need to talk about this."

This! My wanting to have sex with you in my office.

Like the oversexed teenager I used to be! My God, I've never gotten over you, and it took me fifteen years to realize what's wrong with me.

Old pain roared back to life. She *would* brazen it out. "Obviously, tonight I've experienced a residual reaction from the toxins. Otherwise none of this would have happened."

"Possibly," he said with a little smile, but she could see the mockery flickering through his eyes. "I repeat. We need to talk. Go sailing with me again. This Sunday at Belmont. Five o'clock."

She'd never felt so trapped by her own feelings. She wanted to be with him, explore these feelings she'd had forever. But she couldn't, wouldn't make the same mistake again. Long ago he'd said he'd never forgive her, and his actions had made her believe him.

"Drew, this is ridiculously embarrassing for both of us. Let's forget tonight ever happened and go on our merry way like we have for the last fifteen years. We have nothing further to discuss except for the lost Bertha Palmer dresses."

And my father. And all these conflicting feelings I'm afraid will never go away.

"To hell with Bertha's gowns. You know what we need to figure out. Are you brave enough to do it?"

It had always been a mistake to look into his eyes when he wanted something, but she had a lifetime of making the wrong choices with him under her belt. For generations it had been said the Clayworths always got what they wanted.

"Are you brave enough?" he repeated. "What have you got to lose by meeting me?"

My heart!

But in a public place and on his boat the size of a large bathtub, she would be safe enough from making a bigger fool out of herself.

She flung up her chin. "I'm brave enough. Sunday. Five p.m. Belmont Harbor."

"I'll be waiting." He walked out with a saunter that looked way too confident.

Of course she knew it had to be her imagination, but she heard an echo of laughter in the room. She looked up at the heavy moldings, and the carvings really did look like faces. Dread and excitement mingled into an absolute certainty that she'd played right into fate's nimble fingers, and it terrified her. But she'd be there Sunday night to defy fate once again.

CHAPTER 12

On Thursday, Drew stared down at a stack of files on his desk, a slew of e-mails he needed to answer from the crew who would race in the Fastnet with him, and a list of calls to be made to the last three museum trustees, confirming their positive votes for the scholarship fund. None of it went as smoothly or quickly as it should have.

How could it when every few minutes he glanced at the clock, counting down the hours until Sunday. And Athena kept flashing before his eyes. Athena laughing...dancing...singing. He chuckled every time he thought of her off-key warbling.

He forced himself not to dwell on Athena in his arms. The taste of her mouth and skin on his lips.

He needed to go slow. Get used to the idea she'd betrayed him out of love.

There, I've used the word. She thought she loved me.

God knew he'd thought the same about her.

What would have happened if she hadn't told his

uncle about his plan to leave college and go sail in the Fastnet? What would have happened if his family hadn't stopped him with their power and his own sense of what he owed them and his name? What would have happened if he hadn't shut Athena out?

He wanted time to find out. Time to get over the past. Time and distance between them and the trouble with her father.

But time stopped for no man. He'd learned that a long time ago.

Time seemed to be moving in slow motion. But at last Saturday dawned. Today, like every day since the night in the museum, Athena found it hard to think of anything except Drew, and her head filled with visions of what might happen tomorrow that made her blush.

Bertha's toxic boning appeared to be having a lasting effect on Athena. Like Penelope realizing she wanted her ex-husband back, and Shelby wanting to reclaim her love of eating and cooking, Athena wanted Drew. She tried to concentrate on Bertha's two dresses, successfully decontaminated, boning replaced, safe and ready for the exhibit. She tried *not* to think about the remaining two dresses and what might be their fate. The trail had gone cold for her. And by all reports Ed's investigation had come up empty.

Thankfully, today she needed to be at Pandora's Box. *Wanted* to be there to help Venus, who managed the store alone Tuesday through Friday.

She caught a glimpse of herself in the store's glass window and stopped.

I look different. More alive.

To compose herself before her inquisitive sisters saw her

altered state, she bought time by studying the window display. All pure Diana. Elegant but whimsical. A mannequin, wearing a lavender French lace 1940s peignoir and matching nightgown perched at a dark mahogany dressing table with a large center mirror and two smaller ones. Beautiful perfume bottles, a large compact with a heart picked out in red crystals, and a party invitation for a Service Club of Chicago Black Tie Ball lay on the table. Beside the dresser stood a mannequin in a 1947 Dior New Look black and white checked evening gown with an underskirt of tulle and bodice of black cotton lace. On the other side, the third mannequin, in a pale blue 1950s organza dress, fitted at the waist and bordered in bands of pink and yellow flowers, lounged on a slipper chair. They looked like they were talking, gossiping together before they went off to a fabulous black tie affair. Just as she so often did with her sisters.

Taking a long, deep breath, Athena strolled in, ready with answers when her sisters reacted.

The store glistened brighter than ever this morning, like it had been polished to perfection. The ivory satin Valentino gown and matching long coat looked exquisite on the mannequin, welcoming everyone in.

Venus looked up from arranging pieces of jewelry on the round table in the center of the room. Her eyes widened, stretching at the corners.

"Thank God! You got rid of those hideous glasses." Her mock shudder was so over-the-top dramatic, Athena laughed.

Diana rushed through the arch from the other room. "Welcome back, Athena. We've missed you."

"I just took off my dark glasses."

It is so much more.

Feeling guilty, she hugged Diana. In her entire life she'd kept only three secrets from her sisters, and Drew had been the first, and now he was here again.

"I'm glad our old fearless leader is back." Diana pulled away and looked up at her. "We need you. Dad called before you came in, and I let it slip about the robbery and Bertha's gown making you sick. He's upset."

Venus tossed her hair over her shoulder. "Diana, I told you not to say anything about what Dad told us until later."

Fear cooled all the lustful fantasies about Drew.

Did Dad say something about why he's staying away or about his troubles with the Clayworths?

She didn't want to wait. She needed to know the worst now.

She'd heard the worry in Diana's voice and saw the secretive glance between her sisters.

"Tell me now," she demanded.

The shop door opened with its little musical jingle as two women drifted in.

"We'll tell you later," Diana muttered, heading toward the younger woman wandering into the hat and accessories room. Venus turned to the other woman gazing enraptured at the jewelry table.

Athena slipped into the small alcove and dropped her Burberry tote and tried to dump her worry. The jingle of the door opening again sent her back out into the store with no time to brood.

Within an hour, Pandora's Box buzzed with women and one man who came, terror in his eyes, to look for an anniversary present. Half an hour later he left beaming, swinging a gift bag that contained a one-of-a-kind French Art Nouveau brass and black onyx demi-parure necklace and earrings.

Late in the afternoon, only three customers remained sitting in front of the triple mirrored vanity trying on evening hats, little black concoctions of satin and silk, some lined in red, all with whimsical feathers, netting, bows, and French paste ornaments. Athena heard them all laughing as Diana showed them how to wear the hats tilted just so over one eye.

Athena burned to know what Dad had told them. Restless, trying to hide her impatience, she drifted back to the office to check her e-mails. Maybe Dad had contacted her. His usual form of communication. E-mails. No body language. No voice inflections. Nothing to give himself away. Nothing to give her a clue to why he shut her out.

Her iPhone vibrated beside her. Dad's number. Like she'd somehow willed him to call. Or the old bond they shared had been somehow reconnected and he knew she was thinking about him.

For an instant she thought of not answering.

Not today. I don't want to think about Dad and what might have happened with the Clayworths.

She wanted to kick sand in the Fates' faces. Blind them for a second so she could run away again.

No, I'm done hiding.

"Hi, Dad. What a nice surprise." She actually sounded surprised, pleased she could still hide her confusion.

"I missed you earlier. You should have told me about the robbery and about being sick." The note of worry in his voice made her feel so guilty she felt tears pool in her eyes.

I should have called him.

"I'm fine. Really. I didn't want to worry you. Everything's good now. We've found two of the Bertha gowns." Even she could detect the strain in her voice now.

"Are you sure you're all right? Something's wrong. I hear it in your voice."

"No, I'm great. Really. Fine. Honestly."

"This robbery and your illness change things. It's time I came home."

What will that mean for Drew and me?

She felt like a selfish pig. This shouldn't be about her and Drew. This should be about her Dad and figuring out what had gone wrong for him at Clayworth's. But part of her knew this was another barrier, keeping her away from Drew. She tried to hide it.

"Great, Dad. I look forward to seeing you."

"You don't sound like you mean that, Athena." The crisp, hurt tone in his voice couldn't be missed.

She didn't, and the guilt gnawed a hole in her stomach. "Really, we'll all be happy to see you." The little bell, jingling once more as the door opened, saved her.

"I'm sorry, Dad. Customer."

"Go. I'll be in touch. Soon."

She shut her eyes, her heart pounding like a hammer against her ribs.

Why does it feel as if my life is rushing to some grand exposé of lies, love, and larceny?

Refusing to give the Fates the upper hand, she marched into the main room of the store to find a tall woman with a long, solemn face shifting through the evening clothes.

"Hi, I'm Athena Smith. May I help you?"

The woman glanced up and smiled. Athena was startled at how pretty she looked with her eyes crinkled, her mouth curled deeply at the corners and dimples denting each cheek.

"Hello, I'm Dottie Crawford. I saw you and the shop

on *Talk of the Town.* I never miss Rebecca's show or column." She glanced around. "As usual, Rebecca's right. This is so beautiful and unique. She said it was the perfect place to find a wedding dress."

Athena figured Dottie to be in her late forties, early fifties. Second wedding? She gestured toward the mannequin. "This is the Valentino dress Rebecca liked."

The woman shook her head, her low ponytail swishing across her back, but Athena saw longing in her eyes. "No, no, too grand for me."

"You have the height and figure to carry this gown off."

Dottie ran her fingertips over one rhinestone-encrusted sleeve. "It's beautiful, but it's my fiancée's second wedding and we're trying to keep it simple." She blushed, and the color made little gold flecks show in her brown eyes. "It's my first wedding, so Fred thinks we should do it up a little."

"Congratulations. When's the wedding?"

Blushing again, Dottie laughed. "Two weeks."

"Two weeks! We need to get started." Athena went through the long gowns and pulled out two. A Malcolm Starr and a Lilli Diamond. "Let's try these."

While Dottie changed behind the rich brown velvet curtain, the other three customers left, each carrying a small hatbox.

Dottie came out in the first gown and studied herself in front of the large gilt-edged mirror. The Empire bodice studded with prong-set diamantes suited Dottie, and the candlelight ivory duchesse satin skirt of the Starr gown swished perfectly at the bottom.

"What do you think?" Dottie asked.

There wasn't the look in her eyes Athena wanted to see. "Pretty. But we can do better."

Dottie stepped back behind the curtain and Athena's sisters came to stand at her shoulders.

"Bride. First for her. Second for him. Wedding in two weeks," Athena whispered.

Dottie stepped out in the halter-style Diamond dress. The thick cotton lace over the nude underlining of the bodice looked lovely and a little provocative and the ivory silk matte jersey bottom hung beautifully on Dottie, but Athena didn't like it as well as the Starr dress. Neither did Dottie. They all four shook their heads.

"What about the Valentino?" Diana asked. "It would be perfect."

"Absolutely, you must try it," Venus insisted, removing it from the mannequin.

Dottie hesitated.

"Please, just try it," Athena encouraged and felt pleased when Dottie took it from Venus and disappeared behind the velvet curtain.

"I love doing brides," Venus murmured, turning to the jewelry table.

"Me, too," Diana ran into the other room.

Dottie stepped out in the Valentino dress and coat, with the beautiful rhinestone buckle on the belt accenting her narrow waist. Athena gasped. Dottie looked regal, and the expression on her face was the one Athena had been waiting to see.

"I feel beautiful," Dottie breathed, gazing at herself in the mirror.

"You are beautiful." Venus handed her a pair of Vendome earrings, rhinestone-encrusted buttons each with a two-inch drop of pure crystals.

Dottie pulled her hair out of the low ponytail and up into a high knot on her head to show off the earrings.

"You're a size-eight shoe, right?" Diana asked.

When Dottie nodded, Diana helped her slip on satin d'Orsay pumps. "Here, this Charlet rhinestone bag, handmade in France, finishes the outfit off."

"It's perfect," Dottie sighed, still staring at herself in disbelief. "I never thought I could look like this."

Athena got a lump in her throat. "You'll dazzle Fred in this."

"I've felt dazed since I met Fred two weeks ago."

"And you're marrying him already?" Venus gasped, looking as shocked as Athena felt.

"I should have said met again." Laughing, Dottie flushed. "Twenty-five years ago we dated in college and reconnected at our college reunion. Fred's been divorced for years, and I never married. He says we were always meant to be together but we were too young then to deal with it."

"I love when couples get back together," Diana sighed.

Athena sat down hard on the settee.

Lost in thoughts of Drew and *their* past, she watched her sisters fussing over Dottie without really hearing what was being said.

She tuned back in as her sisters presented Dottie with a gift.

Dottie shook her head. "I can't accept these earrings as a wedding gift."

Her sisters chorused, "Of course you can."

"Please. We want you to have them," Athena added.

All of this happened on the outside. Inside, her life played over and over in her head. If she'd needed any further evidence the Fates planned to drag her kicking and screaming toward some monumental conclusion, they'd just given her a preview.

Half an hour later, laden with the hanging bag holding the Valentino dress, and several boxes, Dottie paused in the door Athena held open.

Turning, she smiled at all of them. "Thank you all. I feel like you're my fairy god-sisters." With a wave, the blissful, blushing bride left to live happily ever after.

"Or we're three busybodies, like Mom sometimes called us." Diana laughed.

"Or the three Fates butting into everyone's business," Athena sighed.

"No, we simply love to make people happy." Venus flung herself down on the settee. "Fabulous day."

"Now please tell me why you're worried about Dad," Athena blurted out, unable to wait another moment, now that she realized time was running out.

"We think he's keeping a secret from us." Sadness flickered through Diana's eyes.

Dread gnawed at Athena's stomach where guilt had left off.

"She thinks it's a terrible secret. I don't," Venus shook her head, and thick tendrils of hair slipped out of her top-knot to fall charmingly around her shoulders. "I think it's some kind of good secret. Honestly, Dad hasn't sounded so content in years. Who wouldn't after being freed from those overbearing Clayworths? Of course he didn't sound as great after we told him about the robbery and you."

"Let's go to Florida to see him," Diana declared, hands on hips.

"He's coming home soon."

"What!" Venus sat up. "Did he e-mail you?"

"He called my cell this afternoon to tell me."

"I knew he was worried about you." Diana nodded. "It's time for him to come home. It's time for all of us to put this business behind us."

"For once you're right, Diana." Venus sighed. "I suppose I'll have to put up with the Clayworths, but I'll never forget about this or forgive them for it. I'm like an elephant."

"Life goes on. We need to seize happiness whenever and wherever we can," Athena said with new determination.

Venus sat bolt upright on the settee. "You've met a new man!"

Athena shook her head.

"Yes, you have. I see it in your eyes. They're getting darker. Mysterious." Venus chuckled. "Tell us everything."

"I promise you I haven't met anyone new," Athena declared with real feeling.

"Someone old. Someone you knew before. Like Dottie and Fred," Diana said softly.

Stunned by how close she'd come to the truth, Athena stared at her youngest sister.

A mischievous glint in her eyes, Venus twisted around, flashed Diana a grin, and turned back to Athena. "Mom always thought Diana was a little clairvoyant. Is she right? Who is he?"

"Diana is smart. If it isn't someone new, then it's someone old." Athena lifted her chin to the ceiling. "In my case it's too soon to be talking about romance. We're talking about Dad. If he's coming home soon, we need to make sure the house and yard are in good shape. You know how fussy he can be."

"Let's meet at the house and see what needs to be

done." Venus shrugged. "Sometimes I wish he'd sell the money pit, but it has so many memories."

Both her sisters gazed off into the distance, no doubt thinking of the rambling old house where they'd grown up, with its old wood floors and huge fireplaces, and the great paneled library where their father pored over books on mythology.

"I think we should go have a picnic on Oak Street beach, the way we always did on Sunday evenings in the summer." Diana smiled up at her. "What do you think, Athena?"

"I'm sorry, I can't tomorrow." She thought very carefully how to word this so as not to tell any more lies to her sisters. "I have a meeting about the exhibit."

"How about afterward?" Diana asked.

Rapidly calculating what time the sun set, because certainly she didn't want to be out in Drew's tiny boat after dark, she nodded. "Come to Belmont Yacht Club around seven-thirty and meet me. Too late for a picnic, but we can go to the house."

"Is the meeting with Drew?" Diana asked softly.

Venus swiveled around to look at Diana and back to Athena. "It is, isn't it?" A steely glaze in her eye, she nodded with so much gusto, more hair fell around her shoulders. "I know he's helping you find the dresses and all of that, but doesn't it bother you not knowing what happened between him and Dad? You know how I feel. All Clayworths should go suck a lemon. We'll come save you from Drew at seven-thirty sharp."

If only Diana *was* psychic, then she could tell Athena whether or not she was making another mistake and whether her sisters' arrival would be too late to save her.

CHAPTER 13

On Sunday the cab driver stopped several yards away from the entrance to the Belmont branch of the Chicago Yacht Club.

"This is as close as they let us get."

Athena sat in the back seat, staring out the window toward the lake and the floating gray New England clapboard Yacht Club. She literally could not move, torn between cold, solid self-preservation, the status quo, and hot, fluttering eagerness to live dangerously. Could Drew be her destiny like Fred was Dottie's? Or more likely, would Drew rip out her heart and this time she'd never recover?

"This is the place you wanted to go." The cab driver's impatient tone caused her to look up and catch his eyes in the rearview mirror. He didn't look happy.

"This is the place you wanted to go," he repeated louder, like she hadn't heard him the first and second times.

If she hadn't *really* wanted to come, she'd have stayed

in bed with the covers pulled over her head the way she'd been doing for the past several months.

"Yes, this is the place. Thank you." She paid the meter and threw in an extra five dollars for sitting like a lump, wasting his time.

The cab screeched away, merging onto Lake Shore Drive.

Still, Athena stood where he'd dropped her, clutching her canvas tote. If she and Drew were part of some grand Greek epic, or star-crossed lovers, best to get it over with instead of standing here getting sunstroke.

She meandered along the picturesque waterfront with docks holding boats, some old and classic, others new and sleek. On her right, the dry sail area looked like giant ship models on stands, waiting to be taken down and sailed away.

Now she could see the entrance with the guard dressed in white nautical gear.

Drew burst past him, running toward her. His blue polo shirt and swimming trunks made him look tan and fit.

Damn! He looks too adorably hot. But forbidden.

She clutched the tote to her chest like an anchor keeping her grounded. "Am I late?"

"No, you're right on time." Grinning from ear to ear, his eyes squinting nearly shut from the bright sunlight, he grabbed one of her hands, twining their fingers together. "C'mon, I moved my boat to the edge of the clubhouse."

It seemed rude to insist *unhand me*. But serious self-preservation made her dig in her espadrilles. The white-caps on the lake looked huge.

"The Skokie Lagoons are one thing. Fun. Great. But isn't your Penguin awfully small for Lake Michigan?"

His genuine amusement made her smile back. "Yeah, way too small. We're taking my Wally 80. C'mon, I'm double-parked."

A huge, extremely modern, incredibly sleek boat took up all the parking spaces.

"It's a yacht!"

"Yeah, remember, I race them." He pulled her up the gangway onto a deck of teakwood big enough for a game of ping-pong.

He led her two steps down into the cockpit with a control panel of switches, dials, and gauges, and lined on two sides with wide, heavily padded blue leather benches.

"There are two staterooms and three heads, and that's the owner's aft cabin."

Down a short hall and through an open door she saw cherry paneling and a wall-to-wall bed draped in Clayworth signature blue.

"Did you bring a bathing suit?" he asked, still holding her hand and her still letting him.

What am I doing!

She pulled her hand free of his warm, smooth fingers and shrugged. "I'm wearing it under my clothes. Only a precaution after getting wet last time we sailed. It's too cold to swim in Lake Michigan yet."

"We'll see," he said cryptically, like he had a secret. "C'mon back up."

She followed and watched him toss blue cushions on the teak deck.

"Sit here and relax. I'll motor out of the harbor before I hoist the sail."

Relax? What am I doing here? This is impossible. I'm so wound up if I let go I'll spin right off this boat.

Panic made her grab his arm. "Wait! You said you wanted to talk. Can't we do it here? Not out there."

"We'll talk once we get out of the harbor. Relax," he ordered again.

Recognizing his stubborn locked-jaw look, she faked indifference, dropping down and leaning one elbow on the cushions, like she had nothing better to do than watch him looking like the movie star Makayla called him, standing at the wheel of his ship, sailing off into adventure. Like Johnny Depp in *Pirates of the Caribbean.*

No. Not like Jack Sparrow. Love Johnny. Hated the gold teeth.

To keep her sanity, or at the very least maintain her nonchalant attitude, she dropped her eyes to watch the way the bow sliced through the lake. The fine bubbles and sizzle as the water passed the bow congealed into seahorses playing in the foam.

Fantasy. Like this.

But the past was no fantasy. It had helped to define her. And that fantasy needed to be put in its place once and for all. Tonight the past needed to be put to rest. And there could be no future, because of her dad.

So why did I come here tonight?

As they passed one big bulky boat in the harbor, three teenage boys, one with a blue Mohawk haircut, and a slightly older young man who seemed to be in charge, shouted and waved to them.

Drew waved back. "That's my dad's old Morgan 46. That's Jeff and the kids from the Youth Center I'm teaching to sail. We were out earlier today. It's a tub to sail. I think you'll like this better."

His smile was real. Not the surface charm he gave

the world. It was like the moment he'd let her in at the museum.

I came here to finish what we started there. I came to make love with Drew. No promises. No future.

Instead of being stunned by her hot epiphany, she felt her body truly relax, relieved to let go of the entire pretense.

Maybe her longing could be labeled sexual attraction. After all, what did she really know about this adult Drew except what she'd learned secondhand from her dad and others, and, of course, from his public life as a retail mogul and his reputation as one of the most eligible men in town.

Maybe the Fates were actually doing her a favor. Maybe having sex with him would cure her. He might be a terrible lover. Selfish. Clumsy.

The memory of his kisses swept over her, leaving her weak in their wake.

Okay. Not clumsy. But probably selfish. Wanting everything his way. After all, he was a Clayworth, accustomed to getting what he wanted.

As soon as they cleared the harbor, he hoisted the sail and she felt the boat come alive beneath her.

A few minutes later he motioned her toward him. "Here, take the wheel."

Shocked, she put her hands behind her back. "I don't know how."

"I'll help you."

The boat seemed to be in a rhythmic pattern of rolling and bouncing. To steady herself, she grabbed his outstretched hand and let him settle her between his body and the wheel.

She concentrated so hard on keeping her hands on the

wheel she no longer felt the heaving beneath her. She forgot everything but the wind and Drew, warm and strong, looming at her back.

The farther out they went, the calmer the lake became, and the boat sailed smoothly across it.

"There, all right now," he said softly above her right ear.

"You kept me busy so I wouldn't notice the chop."

Just like you used to do.

She smiled straight ahead, too confused to turn, for fear of a repeat of the night at the museum. Now she needed to buy time.

"You remember my sailing secrets." He chuckled so close his warm breath stirred her hair falling over her right eye. "Ready for that swim? I've found a warm spot."

Curiosity got the best of her, and she glanced over her shoulder at him. "How did you do that?"

"Environmental sensors." He showed her the gauge. "Seventy-three degrees. Warm enough for you?"

"Yes."

He pushed a button and the sail dropped. She watched him flip switches and push more buttons, and as if by magic a swim platform with a shower lowered and a ladder extended down into the water.

"I'm deploying two rafts on tethers to set up a swim zone. The boat will drift, so don't go past the last raft."

She looked around and saw nothing but water and sky, the sun still huge but lower to the horizon and redder.

"Is it all right to just drift out here?"

"I turned on radar and AIS with alarm zones. It's high-tech privacy." He looked deep into her eyes. "If anyone comes along to disturb us, alarms will go off. I've preset a five-mile zone."

They couldn't have been any more isolated. The world focused down to just the two of them. Like in her hallucination. Drew and Athena with nothing between them.

Now here they were, Drew and Athena with years of unrequited feelings, distrust, and the ever-present pain about her betrayal—and now her confusion about the Clayworths and her dad—between them.

She gave a stab at being rational. "Are you ready to talk?"

"I'm ready for a swim." He pulled off his shirt. His muscles were defined, strong, and heavier.

She looked away and pulled off her own tank top and shorts. She'd worn her black one-piece instead of her skimpy bikini, which left little to the imagination.

But his eyes roamed over her and she felt naked anyway. Like they'd been the last time they swam. Naked in the moonlight.

She needed to do something to break the tension wrapping warm bands of anticipation tighter and tighter around her. Sheer preservation forced her to perform a clumsy dive into Lake Michigan.

The cold water struck her overheated skin and shock jolted through her, followed by exhilaration.

All at once Drew surfaced beside her. "Race you to the last raft."

He sounded like he had when they were kids, daring her, pushing her. Laughing, she responded, slicing through the waves in her best crawl. Sometimes, when they were younger, he'd let her win.

Not today.

Today she needed to win on her own, not be given the prize. She stretched out, gave it the last ounce of her strength, speed, and endurance.

They reached the raft simultaneously.

They clung to it together. Her pulse raced from her head to her toes as the waves pushed their bodies closer and pulled them apart.

"It's been a long time since we swam together," he said. "You beat me fair and square."

Still breathless, she almost laughed but couldn't quite make it happen.

"Want to race back?"

"No, you told me to relax, remember?" She pushed away, floating on her back, letting the waves buffer her gently. She tried to enjoy it, but nothing seemed important except Drew and the warm, tingling anticipation of being with him here, now, at last. Right or wrong. Tonight she would make love with Drew Clayworth.

He paddled along beside her, keeping guard, making sure she felt safe within his boundaries. He smiled, his eyes watchful.

She wanted to turn toward him, wrap her body around him here in the water, and pull his head down to open her mouth for his kiss.

"Watch your head," he called out.

Startled, she felt the stern looming over her.

Shivering, goose bumps covering her arms, she climbed up onto the swim platform.

He came up right behind her. "Here, take a hot shower."

He turned it on, and she stepped under the water, loving how it warmed her cold skin.

"Tilt your head back. You have seaweed tangled in your hair." His voice sounded gentle.

The dichotomy of hot and cold made everything seem surreal as she did what he asked.

His long fingers gently massaging her hair felt so sensual she closed her eyes with pleasure.

I don't want this to be just about sex. I want it to be about understanding.

She opened her eyes, stepped away, and turned to face him. "We need to talk, Drew. Now."

For a second he simply stared at her. She didn't know what she'd do if he reached for her. Throw herself into his arms the way she wanted, or push him into the lake the way she should.

Finally he nodded. "I have a robe in the owner's cabin for you. Warm up. I'll meet you in the cockpit."

She hung her wet suit in the head and slipped on the soft blue terrycloth robe. It really did cover her more than her tank top and shorts.

Drew, dressed in black shirt and trunks, must have pushed another button, because a table had appeared in the room where there wasn't one earlier. A bottle of champagne chilled in a bucket, and beside it were cold shrimp, cheeses, and fruit.

"I thought you might be hungry."

She looked at him standing there, gorgeous and charming, and it all seemed too much.

"What are you doing? What are *we* doing? We don't speak for fifteen years. Let me preface that." She lifted her chin and gazed off into space, trying to find the right words in the utter chaos of her feelings.

Her gaze fell deliberately and as coldly as she could muster, considering she felt ready to explode, onto his face.

"You ignore me for years. Then through no choice of our own, we're thrown back together and all of a sudden you're everywhere I turn. Pandora's Box. Finding

Bertha's dresses. Funding exhibits at the museum. Nearly making love in my office, and now *this!*"

He poured her a glass of champagne and handed it to her. "Here, have a drink."

"I don't want a drink," she insisted but took the glass anyway to pace around the room.

"What do you want, Athena?" he asked softly.

She turned to face him, placed the glass carefully on the table and flung up her chin.

"I want to know how you could so easily walk away from me that Christmas weekend," she blurted out.

There! I've finally said it.

Years of yearning, of regret pushed open every door.

She saw herself follow him out to the porch on that long-ago Christmas Eve, press a soft kiss on the nape of his neck because the way he was sitting, so dejected, compelled her to touch him in that way. She remembered kneeling in front of him, tilting his chin up to gaze into his eyes. Saw the moisture on his face, which couldn't have been from the falling snow.

The memories made it hard to breathe, but she forced herself to look into his eyes again.

"Do you remember what I said to you and what you answered that Christmas Eve?" His voice sounded raw, like the words were ripped out of him.

"Of course I remember," she whispered, tears aching in the back of her throat. "You said, 'I'm alone,' and I said, 'No, Drew, you're not alone. I'll always, always be here for you.'"

He nodded. "And then I picked you up in my arms. Like this."

I should stop him.

There was no snow, no icy-cold wind whipping her hair across her face, but the desire felt the same—no, stronger—as he swept her up into his arms, holding her high against his chest.

He walked to the cherry paneling, not the cold stone side of the Clayworth mansion as he had that night, and he lowered her to the floor, pressing her back against the wood.

Now, like then, he dragged his mouth across hers. Gently bit her lips, the side of her throat, while his hands roamed over her body, making her flesh come alive beneath his touch. Her breasts swelled under his palms, and a tingling flow of desire caused her to move instinctively against him.

He slipped his hands inside her robe, like he had under her dress, cupping her buttocks to lift her to him. She'd ached and trembled, and tears filled her eyes. Like now.

"Then I said I love you, Drew. I've always loved you. We'll always be together. You'll never be alone again," she gasped, her mouth moving against his.

Now, like that night, Drew stopped, grew rigid, and stepped back from her.

"You were seventeen, the daughter of valued friends. A virgin. I wasn't. Clayworths, contrary to popular belief, have a code of honor. Honesty in life and work, love of family and friends, and an effort to give something back to mankind. If we had made love that Christmas Eve, I would have betrayed that. You scared the hell out of me, because I didn't know how I was going to take care of myself, let alone take care of you. We were too young, but I trusted you, told you what I planned to do."

She closed her eyes, remembering, like she had countless times, his passionate declaration that he would win the Fastnet for his parents. Her frantic cries that his uncles would never allow him to do something so dangerous, and his cool words, "They'll never know. Only you know, and you'll never tell." Her nod of agreement, even as she plotted how to stop him, how to save him.

She opened her eyes, brave enough, as she'd promised to face this.

He stepped closer. "I believe you told my uncles because you thought you were doing the right thing. You cared about me and wanted to keep me safe."

His simple words, spoken with conviction, penetrated her battered heart. His face blurred behind her veil of tears.

I believe him.

"Give me your hand, Athena."

Blood pounding in her head, she reached out and twined their fingers together, allowing him to lead her to a cushioned bench along the wall.

He flung himself down beside her, his face open to her instead of the charming mask he showed the rest of the world.

"Athena, this is our second chance. If you're willing, let's see where we go from here." His eyes clouded to a slate blue. "No pressure, I promise." Drew shifted closer, and his eyes softened to warm cornflower. "Will you give us another chance?"

She swallowed, trying to rid herself of the urge to break openly into sobs of joy. But if they had any future, there was one more hurdle to cross. She flung up her chin, needing to vanquish the last lie. They had come too far to shy away from the truth now.

"Dad won't tell me what happened at Clayworth's. Why he resigned. Why you let him. Will you tell me?"

He narrowed his eyes so she couldn't read them. "We

all agreed not to discuss it. Including your father. I have to honor that."

Fear and doubt made her weak.

I won't cry. I won't cry.

But she failed. Large, hot tears totally blurred Drew's face mere inches away.

"Christ, Athena, please don't cry. Tell me what you want me to do. How I can help you understand."

His raw voice touched a place deep inside her, vulnerable and waiting. It was enough for now. "Kiss me," she ordered.

He crushed her to him, and she wrapped her arms around him. He kissed her cheeks, her eyelids. He opened her mouth for long, slow kisses and his hands were all over, feeling her through the terrycloth robe. Scorching current ran through her and into him. She pressed her breasts against him, wanting to be closer, to feel every part of him.

They went down together onto the soft bench. He pushed at the robe, freeing her. With her hands trembling, she hadn't known how hard it would be to jerk off his shirt and push down his swimming trunks.

She hadn't seen him naked since she was seventeen. He looked more gorgeous than she remembered, and she felt beautiful as his eyes roamed over her.

She wanted to say something, but she didn't know the words. Something important, more intimate than mere sex was happening to her, and she didn't know how to tell him.

He scooped her up and carried her toward the owner's cabin. She laughed to hide her feelings and pressed a kiss on the nape of his neck where his hair grew in a vee.

He shuddered. "I loved when you did that."

Naked, they fell onto the wall-to-wall bed, rolling over, kissing and rubbing against each other.

He held her down, and eyes wide, she stared at him, heat rising between them.

"I want to kiss every inch of you," he whispered. He pressed one slow, gentle kiss on her bruised shoulder. Moved lower to rub his lips against the fading bruise on her wrist and place a long, lingering kiss on her thigh.

She tried to stay still, but she couldn't stop shaking. With his lips brushing the inside of her thigh, she shifted under his mouth. "Drew, kiss me," she breathed.

He took her head in both his hands and kissed her, open-mouth, slow kisses, and she pressed against him, wanting him on top of her, wanting him inside her.

All at once she heard bells ringing.

"*Christ,*" he groaned, burying his face in her neck. "It's the damn alarms."

"They're five miles away. We have time." She kissed his cheekbones, his hair, his eyes, not wanting to waste a precious moment of this feeling.

"Athena, I'm going to explode in a few more minutes," he groaned. "I want to make this last longer for you."

From the cockpit came a loud mechanical voice blaring out words she couldn't quite make out.

"Perfect. It's my NOAA. The marine weather station. I have it set to come on every hour." He pressed one more kiss on her swollen wet lips. "I've got to find out what's going on."

Her entire body, from her tingling toes to her excited hair follicles, throbbed with sexual frustration. Staring at the cherrywood ceiling, she thought about the day in her office when she looked up at the molding and imagined she heard and saw the Fates laughing. This time they must be under the bed having hysterics.

She threw on her clothes and followed Drew into the cockpit.

Legs wide apart, he stood at the wheel.

The sun had set. There were no stars. The sky rolled dark gray, and off in the distance, lightning flashed through black, billowing cumulus clouds.

"This storm came up unexpectedly," he called to her. "We're going to motor in."

The storm turned the surface of the lake silver. The boat quivered as it dove into trough after trough of turbulent lake and out again.

She wasn't afraid. She saw the hard, almost detached look on Drew's face. Like he welcomed the challenge of the wind and waves and rain and knew he could survive all of them.

Through the pouring rain, lightning, and booming thunder, he took her right up to the clubhouse. "I have to go back to my berth. It's the last one. But I want you out of this storm."

At the gangway, rain pelting them, he caught her in his arms for one last fast kiss. "I'll call you tomorrow."

"I know." She ran down the gangway and into the shelter of the overhanging porch because she knew he wanted her safe. Fear for him, alone, kept her watching him maneuver away, back toward the entrance of the harbor where the bigger boats were berthed.

It felt too new, this sense of another beginning, of discovery, of realizing she'd been waiting for this since she was too young. A steady calm fell over her body and soul. At her core she felt certain she should be here with Drew and from this point on there would never be another mistake, another regret to haunt her. He understood she'd been trying to protect him all those years ago, and she knew in her heart that when her father returned, somehow, they'd work through what happened at Clayworth's and fix it together. Nothing could separate them now. She wouldn't let it. Nor would Drew. This was too right.

A clap of thunder made her jump, and she strained her eyes, trying to make sure Drew had safely reached his berth. She glanced at her watch.

"No!" She flew back toward the gate, realizing her sisters must be waiting for her in this drenching downpour.

At first all she saw was umbrellas. Then she could make out the guard holding a huge green umbrella over Diana. He was gazing at her as men often did, like she must be some ethereal creature come to life whom he needed to protect. In reality Diana was the most resilient of them all. The last to complain. The last to give up.

Beside the guard, Venus held a glorious red Tiffany glass–inspired, oversized umbrella. Athena could hear her arguing with the guard, like a Greek Fury.

"I'm here," Athena shouted, breathless and soaked to the skin.

"Thank you so much." Diana smiled and moved away.

The guard visibly wilted. "You're leaving?" he asked, looking at all of them with dazed eyes.

"Yes. My sister is here now. Bye," Diana waved.

Venus grabbed her arm, pulling her under the enormous Tiffany umbrella, and Athena huddled on the other side.

"It's about time. We're soaked." Venus sighed. "Diana had the guard nearly talked into letting us into the clubhouse to wait in comfort. We were in time to save you, right?"

Athena gave one shaky little laugh. "Yes. Definitely saved by the proverbial bell."

CHAPTER 14

Since yesterday, excitement vibrated around her. This Monday morning the museum glistened, sandblasted by Chicago's July sun, and the lobby hummed with tourists pouring in.

Leonard's "Good morning, Miss Smith," sounded crisper, brightening her day even more than usual. She floated up the marble staircase and into her office.

Edna Keene turned from talking to Makayla and frowned.

Okay, so maybe happiness isn't contagious.

Athena refused to be daunted. "Welcome back, Edna. Isn't it a glorious day?"

"Without a doubt," she sniffed. "I wouldn't miss our staff meeting this afternoon. You've been a busy bee while I've been away."

It didn't sound like a compliment. Athena lifted her chin, waiting for the next shoe to drop. She'd handle it. At last she truly felt like Athena the wise.

"Well, Athena, I've come to tell you that since you acquired the two Bertha Palmer gowns, the museum board has given the green light for your new exhibit and three trustees have called to renew their support of the scholarship fund."

Drew kept his promise.

Overfilling with warm, tingling joy and excitement, Athena beamed at Makayla. Now all her dreams could come true. "I'm delighted. I hope you are, too, Edna."

Even Edna's deep sigh couldn't faze Athena today.

"I've always admired your tenacity."

Then why do you always give me a hard time?

"Will you throw your full support to this?" she asked, hoping for the best.

"We'll see." Edna glanced toward Makayla, who had gone to work in the corner library nook to give them a semblance of privacy. "You know, I was once a gifted intern here myself."

On that cryptic note, she stalked from the room.

Athena *did* want happiness to be contagious. The world would be better for it. All at once, she was wise enough to know how to help Edna.

Athena laughed. "I think Edna gives us a hard time because she'd like to be more involved with the collection, instead of being upstairs, juggling the budget. If only we could find Bertha's last two dresses, we could give her a little dose of truth serum. It might be just what she needs to seize what she really wants."

Makayla giggled. "Awesome idea. Do you think you and Mr. Clayworth will find them soon? I mean, is it hard, like, to be with him because of, you know, the old BFF thing?"

She shook her head, refusing to give in to doubt. "Don't worry about us. We'll find them soon. Mr. Clayworth and I have come to a meeting of the minds."

I wish it were our bodies.

With great difficulty, she kept her voice neutral, or at least as calm as possible considering her desire to be whispering into his ear, murmuring against his warm mouth, and nibbling on his full lower lip right this minute.

The minute Drew strolled into the flagship John Clayworth and Company store, which took up a square city block in Chicago's Loop, he felt its beat. This would always be the living heart of the chain.

By day, the first floor's wide aisles, pillars, and curved glass counters glowed from the chandeliers and the light from the Tiffany dome ceiling six floors above.

With time to spare before his meeting with Connor, he made his way through the Food Hall, a series of large, long rooms flowing one into the other through wide arches.

He stopped at the Confectionery Department's marble countertop to buy Clayworth Chocolate Mints.

Janette smiled at him. "Hello, Mr. Clayworth. Your usual?"

Nothing's usual about today.

He grinned at her. "Throw in an extra box today. Thanks, Janette." Athena had always loved these. The vision of feeding them to her one by one, licking the chocolate off her lips, taunted him.

Janette stacked up five boxes of almond-flavored chocolate mints, and he laid the exact amount of money on the counter.

She looked down at the pile of bills and up at him. "I remember when you could barely see over this counter and you paid me in pennies."

"Yeah, now it's dollars." He laughed. "Times have changed."

"Thank goodness, not at Clayworth's," she said, pride ringing loud and clear in her voice.

It never will if I have anything to say about it.

"You're right, Janette. We're still the same. The customer must be pleased," he said, repeating the store's motto. "And I always am. Thanks."

To work off his excess energy, his frustration at having to wait to see Athena, he walked up the wide staircase instead of taking the elevator to the ninth-floor executive offices.

On the seventh floor he stopped and looked toward the Maple Room. A long line of customers waiting to be seated for lunch stretched out the door.

Drawn to it, he stood off to the side and peered through the wide opening into the paneled room with the blue carpet symbolic of Clayworth's.

Today the restaurant teemed with parents and kids off for summer break. Seeing it full of families reminded him of Christmas and the Chicago tradition of having breakfast with Santa under Clayworth's giant tree.

His family tradition to invite store executives, their partners, and their children to be the first to see the fully decorated tree the night before it opened to the public brought a memory he'd buried long ago. Now he could let it out, savor it.

He leaned one shoulder against the doorframe and smiled, thinking about the first time he'd seen Athena after being gone for nearly eighteen months at prep school and two summers sailing with his parents in preparation for the Fastnet.

That night he walked into the Maple Room and saw her, hair shining, eyes wide, full mouth curled laughing with her sisters, and she'd looked up at him, and his teenage libido had gone on testosterone overload.

A month away from her seventeenth birthday, she'd grown up.

His best friend, his confidante, became the object of his desire.

Christ, his gut ached, remembering.

His personal code of honor set up the boundaries. A year of memories. The year he lost his parents. The year he fell in love with Athena Smith.

He straightened, his shoulders rigid. Last night he'd never felt closer to anyone. Yet he hadn't told her about finally sailing his own Fastnet to banish the last of his guilt and regret. Find closure. Why? For the same reason he hadn't wanted to discuss her dad? Fear. Fear of losing her again.

Charlotte, the longtime hostess of the Maple Room, who ruled with an iron fist and marshmallow heart, came back to the reservation desk and spotted him.

"What a nice surprise, Mr. Clayworth. The family table?"

He saw the round table for eight empty in front of the large middle window overlooking State Street.

"No, thanks, Charlotte. Who's the next big party waiting?"

She glanced out of the corner of her eye toward a harassed woman, bouncing a fussing infant in her arms, two kids resisting the attempts of a grandmother to entertain them while they waited, and a grandfather gazing into space, wearing a polo shirt with the emblem of a country club Drew recognized. Drew figured the poor guy wished he'd gone to the golf course.

"Give them the family table."

Charlotte's lips twitched. "That is very kind of you. Have a good day."

"I already am." He winked and turned away.

From behind him one of the kids gave a shout of joy. Drew felt the same way since last night.

His stride long and brisk, he entered the Circassian walnut–paneled boardroom on the ninth floor. The plush, thick blue carpet muffled his footsteps.

Connor eyed the bag Drew dropped on the table. "Have you got mints in there?"

"Not for you. They're for Jeff and the kids I'm teaching to sail from the center." *And Athena.* "Go buy your own."

"No cash on me. God forbid I be the family member who doesn't pay cash for my candy at Clayworth's." Connor laughed.

"Talk about us being creatures of habit." Drew shook his head. "How many times growing up did we hear that we could charge anything at Clayworth's but we had to spend our own money on candy. I wonder which of our dads thought up that family rule."

"Mine and my mother put him up to it. If it wasn't for Aunt Bridget, I would have been swiping candy from all of you. So. Let's talk about stealing."

He pulled a notebook out of his briefcase. "Ed and I have both questioned Penelope and Shelby. They were both horrified to discover the dresses were stolen from

Clayworth's Secret Closet." A flicker of a smile curled Connor's mouth. "I failed to point out the fact Penelope bought the dress under circumstances that could only mean it was stolen property. However, they're both charge-account customers of long standing, and we all know what that means."

"The customer must always be pleased," Drew said with a crack of derisive laughter.

"Exactly." Connor nodded. "I assured them John Clayworth and Company did not consider them culpable in any way."

Drew leaned toward him. "Did Penelope give you the name of the fence who sold her the dress? We need to get our hands on the remaining two before anyone else becomes affected."

"She gave us a name, but it went nowhere. A phony. Sorry, Drew. So far the gowns are untraceable. Ed is still working on it. I agree having those dresses out there makes us vulnerable to lawsuits. It's still a possibility with both Penelope and Shelby. Although they both are saying exposure to Bertha's dresses has changed their lives in a positive way."

Athena in his arms flashed in front of him. Yeah, life altering.

"I don't believe they'll sue." Drew shook his head. "Clayworth's can withstand any panic, any troubles in the future as it has in the past. But we need to stay on this. Time is running out."

All at once Drew had an overpowering sense of events rushing to a climax. The Fastnet. Clayworth's. Athena.

He needed to see her. Touch her. Christ, his own pain and anger had kept them apart for years. No more.

• • •

Twenty minutes later he parked in the donor lot at the museum. He took the steps two at a time and in four long strides reached her office.

She stood behind her desk talking to Makayla.

"Hello," he called with all the coolness he could muster, considering he was in the throes of sexual longing. He felt like a teenager. Next he'd be shuffling his feet!

They both stared up at him. Easy to read, Makayla widened her owl eyes in surprise, and Athena blushed a rosy stain across her high cheekbones. He saw her try to conceal her reaction by turning away to study her calendar. But he felt her excitement. It matched his own.

"Drew, you must be psychic. I was just going to call you. The board wants to recognize your generous contribution at a black tie dinner this week. We need to discuss the details. Perhaps we could meet later today?"

He didn't miss the playful glint in her eyes. Regret and an edge of panic bit into him.

I leave for the Fastnet on Friday.

Tonight he needed to be at the harbor overseeing the dismantlement of his Wally to go to England.

Regret and desire ate at his gut. "Tomorrow would be better. Say at five?"

Both their iPhones buzzed at the same moment with text messages. His from the harbor.

"The staff meeting," she murmured, then looked up at the ceiling and shook her head, like she saw something.

He looked up, too, but all he saw was a pale cream ceiling and heavy wooden crown moldings that looked exactly like carved faces at three corners.

"Will tomorrow work for you?" he asked, looking for

an excuse to linger, hoping Makayla had a reason to leave them alone for a second. He wanted to pull Athena into his arms, carry her to that red sofa, and make love to her for hours, days, weeks, forever.

"Athena, it's time to go to the meeting." Makayla glared at him from under lowered eyebrows, a tiny diamond twinkling in one. "Bye, Mr. Clayworth. We've got to go now."

Nodding, he backed up, strangely unsure of himself.

"Tomorrow?" he asked softly.

Athena stared at him. "Yes. My place. Tomorrow at five."

"Tomorrow are you going to talk to Mr. Clayworth about the two of you? Now you're going to make him fall in love with you, aren't you?"

Athena stopped in the hallway outside the meeting room and stared at Makayla. She hadn't realized Makayla still had thoughts of vengeance until she saw it in her eyes. "Of course not," she gasped in real shock. "We've put the past behind us to find Bertha's missing gowns."

"That's awesome, I guess. But I gotta tell you there's more going on with Mr. Clayworth, because every time you two are in the same room it has a really hot vibe."

Don't I know it.

Athena tortured herself with the clear and present knowledge that the Fates, once determined to throw her and Drew together at any cost, seemed now equally determined to keep her away from him. Well, they had played their last nasty trick on her. Nothing, and she meant nothing, would stop her from being with Drew tomorrow.

But first, she had to get through this staff meeting and wait another twenty-four anticipation-packed hours.

She kept glancing at her watch as Edna talked about the budget for the coming year. Makayla nudged Athena out of her daydreams so she could make the appropriate response, a pleased smile and a serene glance into Edna's eyes when she congratulated her on receiving the Bertha Palmer gowns from Drew and renewed support for the scholarship fund.

The rest of the board applauded politely.

Back in their office, Athena gave Makayla a hug. "The scholarship will pay for your living expenses and all costs at the Art Institute. It's what you've worked so hard to accomplish."

Blinking her spiky lashes, Makayla stepped out of Athena's arms. "You're so awesome. You made it happen, and I'll pay you back someday."

She squeezed Makayla's hands. "You are by never letting go of your dreams. Trust me, they do come true."

CHAPTER 15

Dreams do come true. Tonight I'm making love with the man of my dreams.

Athena buried her face in Drusilla Junior's warm fur before putting the cat down next to a plate of her favorite gourmand cat food. While the spoiled darling licked up every morsel, Athena fluffed up her bed and closed the gate to the mudroom, which had been transformed into kitty paradise, scratching post, catnip and all.

She turned off her iPhone and unplugged the house phones.

Now I can concentrate on seduction.

Athena drifted through her small carriage house, old-fashioned rooms with wood paneling and fireplaces in the living room and a smaller one in her bedroom.

These rooms, the feel and look of them, had always reminded her of the house where she'd grown up. A mini money pit she'd laughingly called it while restoring the small house to its former glory.

It might be warm tonight, but she loved her bedroom lit by only flickering flames, so she struck a match to start a fire.

The four-poster brass bed loomed as wide as the wall-to-wall bunk on Drew's boat. She saw herself and Drew there on the antique white cotton lace spread, resting on the pile of silk pillows, like they'd been on the Clayworth blue down comforter on the boat. Could smell his clean skin and feel the almost electric touch of his lips.

How would Drew feel about this intimate bower? Too soft, like the Egyptian cotton sheets on the bed?

Would the dressing table with crystal perfume bottles, and the sterling silver hand mirror engraved with her initials, seem too feminine? Would the books in the low bookcase against the far wall help him understand who she'd become in the intervening years?

She felt hot and eager but amazingly calm. There wasn't any pretense. Any fear. They both knew why he was coming here tonight, and they both wanted it.

The old grandfather clock in the living room chimed the hour. Four p.m. Only an hour left.

She ran a hot bath and threw in her favorite bath oil, floral with a hint of spice.

She piled her hair on top of her head with tortoiseshell combs and stepped into the deep claw-footed tub. The perfumed steam swirled around her as she leaned back and closed her eyes.

This is how I prepare to seduce the man of my dreams.

When the doorbell rang at 4:58, the odd thought came to her that it could be the UPS guy or FedEx with some package, and here she'd be standing in the exquisite lavender French lace peignoir and gown from the store, with her hair falling around her shoulders and every inch of her perfumed.

She demanded the Fates give her a break.

She peeked through the lace curtain on the side windows and saw Drew on the front porch. He paced back and forth in front of the door, and his blue eyes, always arresting in his tan face, appeared the tiniest bit haunted by the possibility of defeat.

She slid the robe off. Better to let him know *this* night was a sure bet.

She opened the door and smiled up at him. Still a little hesitant, he stepped in, his gaze roaming over her body. She shut the door behind him and firmly turned the lock.

She felt the current coming from him. Heat. Hesitation. A magical tension. She smiled.

Something very important is about to happen here.

But who would tip the scale? Make the first move?

Me.

On tiptoe, she leaned all her weight into him and clasped her fingers around his neck. Their lips clung together, broke, met again.

Hers ached and burned a little from the hot current flowing between them.

Like he had on the boat, he swept her up in his arms and she giggled, suddenly breaking the tension, making this achingly real.

At last, I'm where I belong.

She buried her face in the curve of his neck, breathing in his clean scent. He smelled of fresh air, and soap, with a hint of lime.

He pressed soft kisses all over her face and hair, and hesitated only one heartbeat before he found the bedroom.

He lifted her up on the nest of pillows and stretched out beside her. A little muscle danced in his cheek and he looked flushed, making his eyes a riveting blue as he ran his thumb over her lower lip, stroked her cheek.

Every nerve in her body came alive.

"Remember what I did when we went skinny-dipping?" he asked softly.

She bit at her lip, trying not to smile, but failed now that she understood his noble reason.

"Of course. You made me *immediately* put all my clothes back on. My ego has never recovered."

His low, intimate chuckle tickled her throat where he pressed a kiss. "Now I want to *immediately* take them all off."

"At last," she sighed. She went up onto her knees, and Drew followed her so they were in the middle of the bed, her thighs pressed against his.

He lifted a handful of her hair and touched it to his lips. "Scented of roses and everything nice," he said softly.

His warm, dry lips opened her mouth—lingeringly, hot—and again, scorching current ran through her. Blood pounded in her throat and in her breasts under the touch of his lips and fingers.

She slid his polo shirt over his head, running her fingertips along his shoulders and down his well-defined smooth chest. She curled her fingers into the waistband of his trousers, releasing the belt and zipper.

She loved the intense, almost amazed expression on

his face as he leaned back on his arms and let her pull off his pants, briefs, and loafers.

He looked irresistible smiling up at her. The long line of his flat belly and strong thighs was gorgeous, and every part of him showed that he wanted her as much as she wanted him.

Her body felt warm and flushed within the thin confines of lavender silk and lace. "I've always been the shameless hussy who wanted to see you naked."

He ran his hand up between her legs, parting the silk. At his gentle urging, she lay down beside him. He cradled her head, rocking his lips over hers. "No, you've always been Athena the wise."

He slid both straps off her shoulders and the gown fell to her waist. "Athena the beautiful." His lips opened against her breasts, and his tongue made slow circles on the sensitive sides.

She couldn't keep her breathing quiet, couldn't stop her body from shuddering. She'd been waiting a lifetime for this.

With one gentle tug, he threw the gown to the foot of the bed. He pressed a kiss on her hot, naked belly, "Athena the wonderful."

More silken kisses on the inside of her thighs. "Athena the perfect." His voice, the one that had always drawn her, made her love him.

Her hips moved against his mouth and he sucked gently, his tongue stroking her.

The sizzling shock released every aching desire, drowning her in him, his caresses, and his hands cradling her hips.

Pleasure built under his mouth stroking her deeper and

deeper, and she couldn't stop the purr at the back of her throat.

"Drew," she gasped.

He slid up over her body, taking her mouth and, at the same instant parting her thighs and pushing inside her in a movement so exquisitely perfect for her needs, her desires, she lost her breath.

Pleasure erupted in waves, one after another. She gripped his shoulders, the tension almost too much to bear. It went on and on until they were both shaking, moving together, one body hurtling through space and time, at last, at last with nothing keeping them apart.

Her face rosy, her hair a beautiful, golden, perfumed silken mess against the pillow, Drew couldn't stop watching her.

In sleep her lips parted a little, luscious and pink. He gave in to his desire to kiss her again. He had years of kisses to make up to her.

"Drew." She breathed his name, like she had earlier beneath him, her face flushed, her eyes glistening. She shifted closer, and he held her safe in his arms. He wouldn't waste a minute of this.

I don't need to tell her now. Later. Later I'll tell her I'm leaving.

Drusilla Junior's persistent meows and her rhythmic scratching at the gate woke Athena during the coldest part of the night.

Beside her on the pillow, Drew slept through it all. In the dim light filtering through the curtains, his every feature made him look like an antique Greek statue, except with astonishing eyelashes.

Where did they go from here? Did they need to talk about the future? What would happen when her father returned soon?

No! I want nothing to mar this new beginning. Later. Later, we'll talk.

She snuggled closer, spooning their bodies together, and promptly fell asleep again.

A tiny beeping sound made her open her eyes and blink. Had she imagined it?

Another tiny beep and she realized it had to be coming from the watch on Drew's wrist, positioned under her left breast.

She glanced at the small clock on her bedside table and sat straight up in bed. "Oh, no, I'm late for Pandora's Box."

He stretched, muscles rippling across his shoulders. "What time is it?"

"Nine-ten."

"Christ, I need to be at Clayworth's."

Both naked, covers tangled around their waists, they stared at each other. Drew had the strangest look on his face, almost disbelief. His eyes were definitely letting her in, and his lower lip looked so kissable she couldn't resist nibbling on it.

"Go! Shower is in the hall bathroom unless you want to join me in the tub."

"Yeah, I do," he growled, nuzzling her neck.

Trying to be mature, she gently pushed him away.

"Can't. Go shower. Meet you at the front door in twenty minutes."

She scurried out of bed, bathed, dressed, and met him in the hallway in record time. She didn't know if she should be embarrassed, or weepy with joy, or if she should try to appear nonchalant.

She'd always been the one who could say something witty in the middle of most long silences. But at the moment, words failed her.

Drew solemnly uttering "We need to talk" broke the spell.

Refusing to let anything spoil this moment, this *pinch-myself-to-prove-this-isn't-a-dream* new beginning, she put one palm over his warm lips. "No. If you're embarrassed, I don't want to hear it. And I certainly don't want to hear that you had a fine time but making love with me wasn't all you'd thought it would be."

She *knew* it wasn't true.

He stopped her nonsense with his lips on her mouth. "Christ, Athena, you're perfect. I'm worn out." He chuckled against her ear. "However, I feel myself reviving."

"Far be it from me to deflate the vaunted Clayworth ego. You were pretty spectacular yourself." Again, she forced herself to be mature and gently push him away. "Now go do good deeds. Call me later."

She watched him run down the steps and climb into his Porsche. Only when the car, with its low roar like a lion suffering a sore throat, rounded the corner did Athena go inside to turn her phones back on and reluctantly return to stark reality.

An edge of concern bit into her bliss when she saw Venus had called her on both phones every five minutes between five and six last night. Plus she'd sent a text demanding to know what Athena was doing and where she was and why she wasn't returning her calls about a lead on Bertha's dresses.

Of course the dresses were important. She shoved away the guilt. Just not as important as being with Drew.

Half an hour later, Athena rushed into Pandora's Box, welcomed by Venus's look of stunned disbelief.

"I can't believe you didn't race right over here when you got my message. I kept Mrs. Strong here for as long as I could last night."

"Sorry. I was buried under unfinished business." She remembered the weight of Drew's body pressing down on her, and hot desire curled through every cell of her body. She took a deep breath and blinked away the image. "What makes you so sure Mrs. Strong is a lead to the Bertha Palmer dresses?"

"She practically described the champagne gown with the train when she was trying to explain what jewelry she wanted to purchase."

"Is she coming back?" Athena mustered interest for her once overpowering need to find the missing gowns. Of course she still worried that others might become infected, but the concern had been buried under her hot anticipation and desire to spend every free moment with Drew, thinking about him, making love to him. The intimacy of two consenting adults trying to build a meaningful relationship.

"I told her I would bring in the perfect jewelry for her, so I could get a promise that she'll be back tomorrow or the next day. I tried, but I couldn't get an address or a phone number out of her. Are you all right?" Venus asked. "You look like you have a fever."

Her core temperature *was* still at a sexual high after hours of bliss, but she couldn't share yet with Venus. She wouldn't understand.

Athena shook her head. "No, I'm fine, really. Just disappointed about Mrs. Strong. But I'm sure we'll get another chance with her." She looked away, straightening a piece of jewelry on the table, trying to appear nonchalant even though her heart pounded and her pulse raced.

Loving Venus, I promise, soon, very soon, there won't be any need for lies.

CHAPTER 16

It had been the longest day of Drew's life. Between Clayworth's, overseeing the transport of his boat, and keeping in touch with Ed about the dead-end investigation into Bertha's dresses, which yielded the fact that they probably would never find the thief, he hadn't seen Athena. Clayworth's would be in Connor's capable hands. He had already changed all the alarms at the Secret Closet and dealt with the police. Drew was half convinced that Bertha's dresses had been destroyed or hidden away somewhere and couldn't hurt anyone else. And finally his boat was ready for its journey to England.

By two o'clock Thursday morning, the mast was down and the keel removed off his Wally 80. His special license in the windshield, Drew followed the trailer to O'Hare Airport in the middle of the night as required by law.

He watched his boat being placed into the belly of a Russian Tubeloff Transport to be flown to England, where it would be reassembled and made ready for the Fastnet.

Tomorrow he'd be joining it.

Today he'd be with Athena again.

After the black tie dinner, they'd go back to her carriage house and make love in her bedroom. So like her. Her breezy charm, her passion for old-fashioned elegance in a sometimes inelegant world.

Then he'd tell her everything. He'd tell her about the Fastnet.

And then he'd tell her he loved her. Had always loved her but had been too young, too stupid, and too afraid to admit it.

Athena sat listening to yet another voicemail from Drew apologizing for being too busy to see her until tonight. Makayla strolled into the Costume Collection office in the middle of it.

Makayla lowered her eyebrows and shook her head so hard her ponytail slapped her on the cheek. "You guys need to talk. Maybe you should write in to 'Ask Rebecca.' I have a friend who did, and Rebecca gave her awesome advice about how guys will tell you anything to get what they want, but it's their actions that show their real feelings." Makayla's eyes widened. "Unless you're taking my advice, after all, and like making him fall in love with you and then dumping him."

Athena felt herself blush and prepared to say something profound. "As much as I appreciate your advice, I decided against it." The extraordinarily determined glint in Makayla's eyes worried Athena a little, but she couldn't discuss the intimate details of her relationship with this young, impressionable girl. Although it was hard not to shout to the world, *Thanks, Fates. Or maybe*

I kicked you in the butt—I'm where I want to be. With the man of my dreams, the love of my life.

She stopped herself, smiled, and uttered what she'd said hundreds of times to her sisters. "Don't worry. I'm sure everything will work out."

Makayla nodded. "Right. Actions speak louder than words. You wait and see."

An hour before the black tie dinner, Athena and Makayla were both ready, waiting in the office to go downstairs to the exhibit hall, which had been transformed as she'd once tried to make Drew see. He still hadn't arrived.

What will he think when he sees me in my black dress? The one I've worn only for him?

Happy Makayla had been here to get her into the dress, Athena smiled into the distance, dreaming about Drew getting her *out* of it.

"Bummer. I forgot my speech for when Miss Keene wants me to say a few words about my scholarship. I left it in the large Collection Room." Makayla jumped to her feet, looking very young and hip in all black and biker boots. "Gotta go get it."

Athena shook her head. "No, I'll go. I'm so nervous I need to walk it off."

Or see Drew a few minutes earlier than planned, dressed in black tie and coming up the staircase.

She didn't see him, but she still floated down the steps, holding her dress by the elegant loop and dreaming about the moment when she would.

Drew, still fussing with his damn bow tie on the way up the staircase, saw Makayla waiting at the top.

"Hello—you look very pretty tonight." He smiled into her watchful eyes. "Is Athena in her office?"

"No. Come with me. I know where to find Athena."

She said it in such a stern, almost angry voice, he worried something might be wrong with Athena as he followed Makayla down into the bowels of the museum, where they'd gone the night they found the first Bertha Palmer dress.

Makayla opened the door, and he saw Athena obviously looking for something on the long table.

He stepped in to help her and heard the door lock behind him. He looked over his shoulder. "What the hell?"

Athena glanced up, a notebook in her hands.

"I believe your young intern locked us in here." Amused more than concerned, he strolled toward Athena. He'd rather be here with her than at any party.

"Oh, no, she thinks she's helping!" Athena rushed past him and tried the doorknob. It wouldn't budge.

"Makayla, it's all right," she called through the wood. "Mr. Clayworth and I need to get upstairs."

"You two need to talk first," Makayla called back, the same note of urgency in her voice that she'd noticed earlier. "You have fifteen minutes before everyone arrives. I'll be back in ten."

Athena sighed, shrugging her beautiful shoulders. "She means well, really she does. The switchboard is shut down. Do you have your cell? I'll call Leonard and get us out of here."

"Now, why would I want such a thing?" Chuckling, Drew prowled toward her.

Laughing, she backed away. "Drew, stop it! You know how long it takes to get in and out of this dress."

"Where there's a will, there's a way." He swept a tangle of muslin off the table and lifted her up onto the edge, so they were gazing into each other's eyes.

He kissed her warm forehead, her fluttering eyelids, and the soft skin at her throat, breathing in her scent.

"What is that perfume?" he muttered, nuzzling the valley between her breasts.

"Jicky," Athena breathed with a little catch. "Supposedly Jackie O's favorite. I should have asked when I saw her at the Secret Closet."

His palms cupped the undersides of her breasts. Below the pit of his stomach, every organ tightened and grew.

"I love it . . . I love . . ."

The door creaked open and Makayla—crying, "I couldn't stop them!"—rushed in, Venus and Diana on her heels.

Athena sucked in a sharp breath, her fingers tangled in his hair, and he froze with his hand cupping her breast.

"Athena, what are you doing?" Diana gasped.

"That's obvious!" Venus stalked toward them. "I'd say unhand my sister, but she appears to be enjoying it."

Prepared to handle this, Drew lifted Athena down from the table and held her protectively behind him, even through she struggled. "Venus, I want—"

"No, Drew." Athena pushed in front of him. "She's right. I should have told them."

"I wish you had," Diana sighed.

Venus tossed her hair over her shoulders. "The road to perdition is paved with good intentions, or some such cliché. You didn't, so now we have this mess, Dad coming home any day, and Leticia Strong in Pandora's Box not half an hour ago purchasing two pairs of Eisenberg Original earrings for two gowns. Shall I repeat that? Two gowns. She doesn't know which one she's wearing tonight. Is anyone else feeling the pressure here?"

He could get both gowns for Athena and protect Clayworth's tonight before he left. He clasped Athena's hand. "Yes. We'll take care of it."

Athena looked up at him, and everything fell in place. Together, they were stronger than apart.

"Yes, Venus, give me the address. Drew and I will take care of this."

"You can't have all the fun," Venus insisted. "I'm going with you."

"No, you're not," Athena ordered. "You and Diana are staying here to represent our family at the dinner."

"And Connor will represent Clayworth's." Drew joined in.

"Joy!" Venus retorted, huffing and puffing and throwing her hair around.

"Don't worry. We'll do it," Diana promised.

"And I'll represent the Costume Collection, right?" Her brows lowered, the tiny diamond barely twinkling, Makayla gazed at Athena. "Are you, like, mad at me?"

Athena's grip on his hand tightened, and the loving smile she gave Makayla spoke volumes.

"Like, I'm not mad, either." Drew laughed, happier than he'd been in, Christ, he didn't remember how long. "Now we'll go find Bertha's dresses and get them here where they belong."

Leticia and Bertrum Strong lived in a crumbling mansion in the midst of overgrown, once magnificent grounds on Lake Michigan, only a few blocks from the Clayworth Compound in Lake Forest.

Athena and Drew had probably sailed past it dozens of times when they were young.

Before knocking on the door, she turned to look up at Drew beside her. Her partner. Her love. "If Leticia Strong has the gowns, we've found them all and no one has gotten hurt."

"I know," He pressed a kiss on the top of her head. "I've notified Lewis. Lake Forest Hospital is ready when and if I give the signal."

I'll never be alone again. We're stronger together than apart.

Knowing it made her tingle all over as she pounded once with the brass knocker.

An older man answered the door, swinging a stunning pair of heavily jeweled Eisenberg Original earrings in one hand, and in the other he grasped the summer dress—black corded gauze with green and pink stripes over green taffeta that Athena had first examined in the top-secret closet.

Standing in the towering foyer, too stunned with relief to speak, Athena felt Drew sigh beside her.

A sound from above caused all of them to look up.

Leticia Strong glided down the sweeping staircase, wearing the champagne velvet gown Athena had lain beneath for an hour to become intoxicated with truthfulness.

Glassy-eyed like Shelby had been, Leticia appeared not to see anything but Bertrum, who gazed at her with complete and utter adoration.

"Bertrum, I love you. I've always loved you, but I was too stupid to know it. I want to be together again."

Bertrum, visibly shaken, muttered, "Leticia, you haven't looked at me like this for seventeen years."

Leticia threw out her arms. "Honey bunny!"

Letting the earrings and dress drop to the floor, Bertrum stepped toward her. "Twinkle-toes! Shall we go up the golden staircase together again? It has long been my fondest wish."

"Yes!" Leticia threw herself into his waiting arms.

Tears stung Athena's eyes. Really, she should do something, but she wanted them to have this moment of bliss.

"I know, Athena, I want them to have this moment, too," Drew whispered as if he'd read her mind, shared her feelings. "But we should do something."

With real regret, Athena tried to get their attention. "I'm sorry, but you really shouldn't be doing this in those clothes."

Leticia, her chest heaving with emotion, turned absolutely clear eyes on her. "My dear child, this is exactly what we should be doing. Life is short, and our fates are in our own hands. We can't recall our past choices, but we can learn from them. Seize the day, dear child. Seize the day! I certainly plan to do so from this moment on. Honey bunny," she murmured, throwing herself back into Bertrum's waiting arms, and they embraced with all the gusto of lovers half their ages.

The ambulance sirens were right outside on the circular driveway. Drew opened the door for them.

"We've dealt with this before," Athena told the paramedics, who were staring at Bertrum and Leticia locked in a passionate embrace. "Just give us the gloves and masks and stand back."

She threw a set to Drew, who, grinning from ear to ear, suited up and surrounded the couple with her.

"Leticia, we must go to the hospital now," Athena called loudly, trying to get her attention.

Bertrum looked up, Leticia's red lipstick smeared all over his face. "Are we playing dress-up again?"

"Yes." Drew gripped his arm. "You lie down here on this stretcher and watch."

"And you be the nurse over here." Athena, holding Leticia's hand, helped her onto the second stretcher. Athena placed the blanket over her. "We need to change your dress now, Leticia. Here, let me help you."

Athena got the heavy champagne gown safely in plastic. Drew had already wrapped the black dress Bertrum had dropped on the floor.

"Remember, twinkle-toes, you dressing up for me used to be one of our favorite games," Bertrum chuckled, turning his head to gaze at his wife, who blew him a kiss as the paramedics wheeled her out the door.

She and Drew watched the ambulances roar away, sirens wailing. "That was the most..." Words failed her, and she laughed until she found her voice again. "*Outrageous* display of love reborn I've ever seen. Thank goodness for Bertha's toxic stays."

"I couldn't agree more." Drew stripped off her mask and gloves. He pressed two long kisses on her open palms and gazed up at her with such mischief in his eyes that she laughed.

"Athena, may we please go up the golden staircase together again? It has long and shall forever be my fondest wish."

CHAPTER 17

She couldn't get him home fast enough.

The instant they walked into her bedroom, she grasped his tux shirt and one by one loosened the mother-of-pearl studs.

As each stud fell to the wood floor with a little *ping*, they both laughed.

She knelt to nuzzle her face into his firm belly.

He gasped. "Athena, stop. I'll never last the ten minutes it takes to get you out of that damn dress."

She looked up into his face. "Where there's a will, there's a way."

His skilled fingers were already moving over her back, undoing buttons. "Thank God, I've always been a quick study."

"At getting women out of their clothes in record time?" she chuckled, unzipping his trousers.

"It's the first thing little Clayworth boys are taught." He slid her dress off her shoulders and her breasts fell free.

His arms were around her, lifting her high on his bare chest so he could meet a sensitive nipple with his tongue.

She pressed closer, wanting more. Wanting him.

Cradling her head, he gently laid her on the bed, her hair cascading over the pillows and his arm as he stretched out on his side.

Maybe it was the profound joy she'd seen on Bertrum and Leticia's faces, or maybe it was the culmination of wanting this man, like this, for most of her adult life. Getting it, and finding him, this intimacy, everything and more than she had ever hoped, dreamed, fantasized about.

Everything about Drew was so sweet to her senses it made her head reel with pleasure.

Each chiseled bone in Drew's face relaxed into tenderness. His hands drifted over her body, freeing her of the heavy dress.

His fingers stroked her wrist and shoulder where the sailing bruises had faded into her pale skin. Stroked across her breasts, down her rib cage to her stomach and below.

"Like a goddess, but not a statue. Warm, loving Athena." His husky voice warmed her lips as the heel of his palm kneaded her until her thighs parted and she arched into his hand and mouth, bringing a tighter, brighter passion than before.

Their gazes locked, his mouth hovering above hers, and with a slowness that felt like liquid fire, he entered her.

The pattern of her breath changed, and so did his.

Their other night of love had been as close to perfect as she'd dreamed. But this, this exquisite fit of their bodies, burned like a fever. They moved in primal rhythms, each sensual motion so tender, so loving, she closed her eyes and lost track of herself. There was only this power they created together.

Like Drew had done his whole life when he knew he couldn't under any circumstance oversleep, he woke every hour on the hour to check the time and to kiss the closest part of Athena he could reach.

When he awoke the next time, he shifted down to lay his cheek under her breasts, listening to her heartbeat. He felt at peace.

He tightened his arms around her and pressed his lips into the Jicky-scented warmth between her breasts and called her name, "Athena."

"Yes, I'm here," she whispered and ran her fingers slowly through his hair.

"I have to leave you in the morning. I'll be away in England for a week or so."

He felt her stiffen in his arms, and he shifted higher so he could see her face. He could always read her feelings in her eyes.

Her eyelashes were a dark fringe as she looked down and then up at him, staring with an intensity that demanded answers. "Why are you going to England?"

"I'm sailing in the Fastnet." He said it as quick as he could. She of all people knew what this meant to him. To them.

"Why?" He heard the tears in her voice, saw them glisten in her eyes. He pressed his lips there, tasting the salt.

"They sailed in that race because of me. I wanted it. I should have been on that boat with them. By racing in the

Fastnet, I'll have closure. Be at peace with their choices and mine." He spoke aloud the guilt and pain he'd held close to him for fifteen years.

"Drew, there are other ways to honor them." She shivered, shaking so much he knew he'd said too much, too soon.

He never wanted there to be another secret between them. He tried to hold her. "Athena," he breathed.

"Light a fire first," she whispered.

He flung back the covers, went to the fireplace, and found the long matches on the mantel to light the logs.

The blaze cast strange long shadows across the room as he crawled back into the bed.

He wrapped his arms around her and pressed kisses on her sleepy eyelids, her warm throat. "Don't worry. Everything will be fine. I'm catching a plane to England at nine tomorrow morning. Just a few days. Then I'll never leave you again. I promise."

He didn't know how long they snuggled under the covers, kissing each other all over while he murmured that he meant his promise, they'd wasted too much time, she was perfect, wonderful, and he could never have enough time with her. Athena permeated his body and mind. He felt panic, like this night was momentous and he had to hold her tighter and make love to her hot, sleepy body and fascinating mind.

Athena's mind raced with feelings and images of Drew and the Fastnet and his leaving her. How could he? They had just found each other again. She wanted to understand his need to finish the race that his parents had never completed. His words had torn at her heart.

She tried to hang on to these feelings but they faded beneath his slow, sweet kisses, which went on and on. His intimate words spoken amid the soft sheets filled her with so much longing she felt tears well up in her eyes.

Drew had always been the reason she could never feel this with anyone else. Why she'd always felt like she was making a mistake with another man. It had always been Drew. Drew in her heart and mind.

The leaded-glass windows with the stained-glass panels on top reflected the firelight, causing a prism of color to play across their bodies. His looked so beautiful and strong to her. So precious she never wanted to let him go.

"I love the weight of your breasts in my hands," he whispered.

She thrust to meet him, wrapping her arms, her body around him.

His voice, his husky sounds of desire, of wanting her, released something wild. She opened herself to him completely. With them there weren't any inhibitions or pretense.

He rolled on top of her, the crush of his weight, him hard against her, driving her a little mad.

I won't let him go.

She felt so hot, so full of love for him she knew she would explode any second. She lifted her hips, welcoming him inside her.

She withered under him, shuddering with each of his powerful thrusts. Rigid, heat pumping through him into her, Drew called her name and she held him. The overpowering sensation of being filled, complete, caused sobs of joy in the back of her throat.

Like the Greek Sirens, Athena would call his name, hypnotize him, bind him to her so he could never leave.

She held him tight, feeling his warm breath against her breasts.

She held him until she knew from his even breathing he had fallen asleep. She pressed one more kiss on his forehead and slowly, carefully eased away from him.

The way his face looked in the firelight, the high cheekbones, the long, full curve of his lips, brought fresh tears to her eyes. It felt like a weight pressing down on her chest now that she understood what racing in the Fastnet meant to him. But what might it cost him?

She'd been waiting her whole life for these nights with him. To show with her body what she'd always felt in her heart and mind for Drew. To have had this intimacy for so short a time and to have it be over at dawn reminded her of the worst of all the Greek tragedies her father had taught them. So many nights wasted, and more to come.

Logically she knew he would be away only a few days.

When his parents went to the Fastnet, they never came back.

She padded stark naked into the small office. The light from the computer screen flashed three a.m.

She googled the Fastnet.

It was all there, the articles about the famous offshore yachting race. Particularly the Fastnet the year Drew's parents were killed. The words conjured up the waves in the Fastnet storm big enough to capsize large and small boats alike. She could *feel* the frigid night with roaring white water surrounding her. *See* the rudder of Drew's parent's yacht snap off and the violent waves throw the crew out of the cockpit to the end of their tethers into the freezing, deadly ocean.

She switched off the computer and sat staring at the blank screen. The course of her life had altered because she'd been forced by circumstances, fate, to reveal her true feelings. Drew, too. She knew it, felt their unique bond forge in a new, more powerful way. She couldn't, *wouldn't* let him sever it again. She'd keep him here any way she could. Make love to him all night if necessary. She smiled into the darkness—no hardship there. Any thoughts that he might be a selfish lover were laughable.

This feeling rivaled the stuff of legend, of myth. Maybe she was being silly. Giddy and stupid on love.

No way would he be getting on that plane tomorrow morning to sail in the Fastnet. She'd convince him to never go.

She'd stopped him once. She'd do it again to save him.

She went back into her bedroom and crawled into the bed next to him.

CHAPTER 18

When Drew opened his eyes, Athena lay beside him, her face dreamy in the flickering light. She curled up against him, and he pulled her closer. She felt petal soft and smelled of Jackie O's perfume and him.

She kissed him in a soft, drunk-on-love sort of way, and he couldn't resist doing the same. She felt too good.

The hot tension started building up inside him. Christ, he wanted her again. Even though he could hardly keep his eyes open, he fought sleep with everything he had.

He needed to make love to her one more time. Before he left, he'd tell her he'd always loved her but was too stupid, too young, and too afraid to admit it.

The sound of the shower beating against the bathroom tiles woke Athena. She sat up, shivering alone in the bed. Her Bose clock radio blinked five a.m. Obviously, she hadn't tired him out enough. Too early.

I need more time.

When she opened the glass shower door, Drew was soaping all over, his beautiful hands sliding down his body, like she wanted to do.

She stepped under the torrent of water and took the soap from his hands. Slowly, she rubbed the fragrant sandalwood bar over his shoulders, down his flat stomach, between his thighs. She lingered there, gliding her hand over and over, feeling him swell beneath her fingers.

"Athena, stop it," he said with a shaky laugh.

"Don't you like it?" She widened her eyes the way people do when they're daring someone.

"I like it too much," he gasped, reaching down to take the soap away from her.

Smiling, she let him remove the bar from her fingers. She slid to her knees and put her mouth where the bar of soap had been. The water flooded over her hair and face as she licked the contours of his body, sucking gently, all the while stroking his hips and thighs with her hands. She loved the feel of him, filling her mouth, her palms.

"Christ!" He pulled her up into his arms, and she wrapped her legs around him. The water felt cool against her hot body as he pushed her against the cream tile and plunged into her until she felt too weak to do anything but cling to his slippery body, loving the feel of him inside her and his mouth open and gasping against her throat.

Afterward he wrapped her in a large, soft green bath sheet, drying every crease and valley of her body. He carried her to the bed and lay down beside her, folding her into his arms.

"Christ, Athena, I'm a mere man. I'm exhausted," he sighed, kissing her lips.

"I told you I've always been a demanding hussy," she murmured, her head on his shoulder.

"And I love every nanosecond of it. What do you command now?"

"Go to sleep for a little while." She kissed his shoulder. "It's early yet."

"Yeah, but don't let me nap more than fifteen minutes." He yawned and closed his eyes. "I love you," he murmured, already half asleep.

"I love you," she whispered back.

Ripped in two between fear and love, she drew up her knees, ran her fingers through her damp, tangled hair, and watched him sleep.

When the clock reached the appointed fifteen minutes, she wanted to throw it in the closet or drown it in the bathtub. Stop time.

So much precious time had passed with them apart because, torn between love and fear, she'd betrayed his trust. She could do it again.

He'd been young and vulnerable then. But he wasn't an impetuous boy now, nor she a naive, terrified young girl.

She touched his shoulder. "Drew, it's time to go."

He opened his eyes and blinked. Turning his head, he gazed at her with such open trust, she knew in her soul that she hadn't made a mistake.

"I hate leaving you."

"I know. Do you want me to drive you to the airport, since you left your Porsche last night for Connor?"

"No, the driver will pick me up here, stop at Clayworth's for my luggage, and then go on to the airport." He gave her one quick kiss and flung back the covers.

"The only way I'm getting out of here is to take a cold shower."

"And I'll go make you hot coffee." Trying to be mature when she wanted to launch herself into his arms, she threw on a silk robe instead.

She heard the shower as she padded toward the kitchen. The doorbell ringing stopped her.

The driver had arrived early. No sense in hiding the obvious. Athena opened the door.

Tall, his pure white hair still as thick as a sable pelt, eyes the identical aquamarine of hers and her sisters', Athena's father stood staring down at her.

"*Dad!*" Athena gasped, clutching her robe tighter across her chest.

"I know it's early, but I landed an hour ago and I wanted to come here first to see for myself that you're all right." He lifted one thick eyebrow. "Aren't you going to let me in?"

"Athena, have you seen my wristwatch?" Drew, his tux shirt hanging open over his trousers, wandered down the hall.

His eyes locked with her father's, and all the oxygen seemed to be sucked from the room.

Drew recovered first, coming closer, buttoning his shirt. "Hello, Alistair."

Her father nodded and stared down at her.

She felt totally vulnerable, but she flung back her head and returned his gaze, searching his face for answers.

"I'm with Drew, Dad," she said simply.

"I see that. I've interrupted. We'll talk later."

"No, Dad, wait!" She reached out to stop him, but he didn't turn, his back ramrod straight.

The door swung shut, and she stared at it, dazed with disbelief.

She swayed back, and Drew caught her in his arms, holding her. She turned, burying her face in his chest, and soaked his tux shirt with her tears.

"I can't believe Dad found out this way," she shuddered, trying to breathe between her sobs.

"I'll talk to your dad. Make him understand."

His voice sounded so full of warmth and love, she believed he could make anything happen.

"Yes." She looked up at him through her tears. "We'll fix whatever's wrong between you and my dad. Together, we'll make this right. All of it."

He cupped her wet cheeks in his palms and stared into her eyes. His were so brilliant, and open like she'd never seen, even when they were making love.

"I love you, Athena. I want a life with you. A life based on truth and trust. You hurt me for what you believed to be the right reasons, and it separated us for years while we grew up. I don't want something I did for what I believe to be the right reason to tear us apart."

His fingers tightened around her face. "We can't fix what happened with your dad and Clayworth's. He's guilty of going outside the boundaries of his fiduciary responsibilities. Then he went further to make up his losses. Took bigger financial risks than he should have, and it put the store in jeopardy. Mine was the deciding vote to reprimand him and demand his resignation."

The warm air in the hall became frigid. Drew had said she wasn't a statue. Now she might have turned to stone.

"But he can't be guilty of doing that. You know what kind of man my father is. The years he devoted his life to Clayworth's. How could you have voted against him if you weren't absolutely sure?"

"I am sure, Athena. The only other people who could have signed off on the transactions are my family. I know none of them would have done this."

The truth slammed into her.

Clayworths closing ranks. Standing shoulder to shoulder.

I can't fix this.

"Oh, yes. The famous Clayworth family loyalty." Her voice cold, her body shivering, she pulled away from him. "So to protect them, you made my father the scapegoat. When were you planning to tell me? Why *didn't* you tell me when I asked you on the boat?"

"I was afraid it would tear us apart before we had this second chance."

She knew the truth was doing exactly what he'd feared.

All the joy she'd felt withered into a hard, cold stone in her chest.

"You're right. It has—I don't know how to fix this. You're a Clayworth. You'll never turn against your family. And neither will I."

"Christ, Athena, you know we can work this out somehow. Not let it come between us. We've come too far to let this happen." He reached for her, but she flinched back, drawing her robe tighter around her like a shield.

The doorbell rang again. This time she knew it must be the driver.

"You need to go." She turned her back on him.

"Come with me!" He pulled her around to face him. "I want you there. I need you there. We'll work this out."

She closed her mind and heart to the anguish in his eyes, his voice, too filled with her own. "How, Drew? I know Clayworths always stand together no matter what. So do Smiths. I'll never believe my father did anything wrong, and you always will. How can we be together with that between us?"

His fingers bit into her arms. "I'm not leaving. I'm staying here. To hell with the Fastnet. To hell with everything except you."

For one beat of her heart she believed the Fates had brought her to this moment to save him again. But she was wiser now and knew she had a choice. She needed to let him go, find his own way, like she needed to find hers.

"You need to go, Drew. I *want* you to go. Now," she said softly, pulling away from him.

His gaze bore into her. "Promise me that you'll be here when I get back?"

"I can't. I'm not sure of anything except that I will never again make you a promise I can't keep."

CHAPTER 19

At Clayworth's, Connor sat in the office that had once belonged to his dad. He cast one long look at Drew's tux trousers and open shirt and smiled.

"I see you had your own party with Athena while you threw me to the lions."

"I need the G-V to get to London. I missed my flight, and I need to get to Cowles. I'm not going on a business trip. I'm racing in the Fastnet." Drew blurted out the truth.

Connor shot him another long, narrow look and picked up the phone.

Full of pain, Drew paced to the window and back. He caught a few words of Connor's conversation with Bridget and then obviously with the pilot, before Drew paced back to the window. Despite his life falling apart, he had to go. Athena was right. His decision about the Fastnet, his belief that he'd never escape the guilt of not being with his parents, had to be put to rest.

Now coldness made him stop and stare blindly down at the famous Clayworth Clock below. Clayworth tradition. Clayworths standing shoulder to shoulder. Did anything matter now that he'd lost Athena again?

A commotion at the door turned him around. Bridget rushed in. "What are you boys up to this time!"

"I'm going with Drew to the Fastnet," Connor said. "Aunt Bridget, you can run this place better than the both of us." Connor shook his head. "Drew, you didn't believe I'd let you do this alone, did you?"

An hour later they were in the G-V, the pilots ready to take off, the second crew required by the FAA for a trip from Chicago to England seated in the crew rest area.

As always, Connor strolled to the forward cabin and immediately started working, and Drew prowled to the galley, poured himself a neat scotch, and tossed it down his throat before he strapped himself in for the flight.

The second or third scotch didn't kill the ache in his gut. This was a different pain than he'd felt that Christmas night on the terrace when he'd left Athena. He'd been too young to understand the loss and loneliness of what he'd decided should be their future. Now he did.

He stared out the window, seeing Athena's face when he'd left her this time and her voice saying, *We can't fix this.* Shutting the door on their future.

Athena cried herself to sleep.

Only Drusilla Junior licking her face roused her out of bed. She glanced at the clock in disbelief. She'd slept the day and most of the night away, exhausted by grief and hours and hours in Drew's arms making love.

No, I won't think about it.

Raw with pain, Athena forced herself to go through her daily ritual. But the bathwater scalded her skin, and then her clothes felt too heavy on her body. Every part of her ached.

She conjured up every lesson on life, on courage, her parents had ever taught her. Her oldest-sister role, stiff upper lip, leader of the pack, had gotten her through most tough times in her life. Doing it about Drew might be the proverbial straw, but she needed to try. Even if they didn't have a future, she couldn't let go of her fear for Drew and what the past might cost his future.

The doorbell rang at an hour barely civil. For one insane instant she thought it might be Drew.

Torn between so many conflicting emotions that she felt sick, she stood and stared at the door. She couldn't fake anything at the moment.

As it rang again, she peeked through the lace curtains to see who wouldn't give up.

She flung the door open for her father.

"Your phones have been off for twenty-four hours. I've come to apologize."

"Dad, I'm the one who was wrong," she sobbed, throwing herself into his waiting arms.

How could she have any more tears left? Obviously a renewable resource, they poured down her face as her father led her into the living room, sat beside her on the blue velvet settee, and encouraged her to cry on his shoulder.

"I've been a fool trusting Drew again. Believing I can fix everything. I'll never forgive him for believing you guilty of…of…of wrongdoing. And not telling me about it."

"I didn't do anything wrong, Athena. I've apologized to your sisters for running away to lick my wounds instead of talking this through with all of you. I thought I was sparing you, but obviously I was wrong."

Her dad's calm voice shocked her into sitting up to stare into his face. "If you aren't guilty of anything, why didn't you stand and fight like you taught me to do?"

His smile gentle, he took out a white handkerchief like he'd always kept in his trouser pocket since they were kids and wiped her wet eyes and nose. "I chose to accept early retirement because I considered Drew's grandfather an old lion whom I greatly respected. To fight would have compounded the problem. There is trouble brewing at Clayworth's, but not of my making, even though the evidence speaks to the contrary."

Justice for her father burned away a small sliver of her grief. "We'll fight it, then. Clear your name with Drew and the others."

"Time will do that for me, Athena. For too long I've let this blight my life. I don't want it to blight yours any longer. I don't want to be the cause of any more unhappiness for you."

"How can I be with Drew when he believes you capable of larceny?"

"Athena, the evidence certainly supported the possibility. I'd consider it myself if I didn't know better."

"He didn't confide in me. Share it with me so we could somehow work it out. Although I don't think that is possible." She couldn't keep the pain out of her voice.

"Why didn't he share his feelings about me with you?"

Burning with embarrassment, regret, she shook her

head. "He *said* he was afraid if I knew how he'd voted I wouldn't give our relationship a chance."

"Would you have?"

"Of course not. I'll never betray you, Dad."

Her father nodded and wiped a fresh tear off her cheek. "Do you love Drew?"

She'd had enough of hiding the truth. "Yes. I've loved him since I was seventeen. But how can I be with him and support you?"

"Drew did what he believed to be right. There are troubles ahead for Clayworth's. Drew will need a woman like you at his side."

Drew's words, *I need you there,* rang in her ears.

"I know you believe in me. You being with Drew won't change that. Make the wise decision, Athena. Choose happiness. Follow your heart with Drew. It doesn't diminish your love and trust in me," her father said softly, love in his eyes.

What would I do if I were still under the influence of Bertha's toxic stays, being given another dose of truthfulness?

Athena knew exactly where the Clayworth executive offices were located on the ninth floor.

They appeared deserted. "Hello," she called, a little edge of panic in her voice.

Bridget strolled out of her office. "Athena, what's wrong? You're as pale as a ghost."

"Where is Drew? I must see him." Fear that she'd be too late made her catch her breath so she wouldn't burst again into loud, sloppy tears.

"Connor e-mailed that they landed in Stansted and

drove to Cowes. That blasted Fastnet begins tomorrow. Damn foolishness, if you ask me. Drew always was the most stubborn of the lot."

Athena gripped Bridget's cool fingers. "Please help me to get to him before the race."

Without any questions, Bridget picked up the phone, and in a few minutes Athena had a first-class ticket on the next flight out.

Hanging up the phone, Bridget winked. "Sometimes it's all right to throw around the Clayworth weight."

As the fleet of boats sailed from Cowes, dawn broke high in the sky. One moment a faint flush on the highest peaks of the clouds, the next, light. The Fastnet had begun. The moment he'd waited for had finally come.

Over the years he'd learned how the sea had many voices. Today he listened to the wind and waves. The hollow booming and heavy roars. The great watery tumbling, long hisses, and sharp reports, splashes, whispers that might be half-heard voices of people at sea.

In the early hours of the race he heard his dad's voice, over and over again. *"No, Drew, you can't come with us."*

He'd come for closure because he hadn't been there, standing shoulder to shoulder with his dad like Clayworths always did. Now he would finish the race for him and his mother.

He heard Athena's young voice. *"Drew, you're not alone. I'll always, always be here for you. I love you. I've always loved you. We'll always be together. You'll never be alone again."*

In the darkest part of the night he heard her woman's voice. *"We can't fix this."*

They rounded the Fastnet Rock off the west coast of Ireland and back to England. The winds were good, strong and cold on his face, calling to him like they always had. Now they were taking him back to England, the finish line of the Fastnet.

His debt paid. A sense of peace about his parents; their choices and his own washed over him. At last he closed the door on the past.

He'd *never* close the door on Athena. He needed her, loved her, and nothing, not Clayworth loyalty or Smith loyalty, would keep him away from her.

Athena knew the instant she saw the deserted docks at Cowles that she'd missed Drew. The Fastnet fleet had sailed.

Fear drove her to ask everyone she could find for news, a way to reach him, tell him she'd come.

Late in the day she felt adrift, weighed down by fear and regret, but she refused to give in to it. Every few minutes all day she'd watched the sky, willing clouds, rain, anything but fair winds away.

Finally she headed back to the hotel Bridget had booked for her to find someone, *anyone,* who could help her.

Connor stood waiting for her in the small lobby.

"I couldn't believe it when Aunt Bridget told me you were here. Why the hell have you come?" Connor's eyes blazed at her.

Hers blazed right back. "Because I love Drew, and I want to be with him whether you like it or not. If you aren't here to help me, get out of my way so I can find someone who will."

She shoved past him.

"Wait, Athena." Connor touched her shoulder.

Her chin jutting to the low oak ceiling, she turned back to him.

"They've already rounded the Fastnet Rock and are heading to Plymouth."

Tears sprang up in her eyes, making Connor look blurry. "Thank God, it's almost over. How can I get there?"

"There's a chartered jet taking a few of us to the finish line, but it's booked solid." He ran his fingers through his hair and studied her with his lawyer look. He reached into his pocket and thrust a white form at her. "Here, take my pass. I know Drew would rather see you at the finish line."

In Plymouth, Athena waited with the crowd, cheering as each yacht sailed into the harbor. She raced to the dock, fighting past other women greeting their men home from the sea.

She twirled around, not sure which way to look, where to go. She swung back to the pier, and there at the end, she saw him.

Like Daniel Day-Lewis in *Last of the Mohicans*, she raced toward her love, except without causing any bodily harm.

Only in the case of the two unfortunate men—one carrying fish, the other cleaning them—that she accidentally knocked over so they both lost their footing and most of their catch ended up back in the sea.

The commotion got Drew's attention. She couldn't see his eyes, but she didn't miss the powerful movements of his body as he raced toward her.

Among flopping fish, their slimy parts, and men cursing in at least two languages, Drew pulled her into his arms, kissing her with a passion that honestly made her light-headed.

"You're here."

She smiled through her tears. "I love you. Despite everything."

He held her tighter. "I'm never letting you go. To hell with family loyalty. Yours and mine. If it takes another fifteen years, I'll convince you we can fix anything together. Believe it." His eyes told her he meant every word.

She clung to him, smelling of dead fish, and laughed when he swept her up in his arms. "I do."

EPILOGUE

Opening night of the Founding Families Exhibit, highlighting Bertha Palmer's exquisite gowns, had been promoted by Kathy Post's PR firm as the black tie affair of the season.

Beside Athena, Drew, not the winner of the Fastnet, but the winner of her heart and soul, stood with his arm draped around her shoulder.

Just as Athena had wanted, people were laughing, dancing, and congratulating Makayla on her scholarship and the museum on the brilliant exhibit. Chicago society at play to support a worthy cause.

Dazzling in a red Valentino gown, Rebecca strolled everywhere, covering the event for both the *Journal and Courier* and her television program.

Her husband, David, stood to the side of the room, talking to Dr. Harry Grant, Kate Carmichael, and Athena's father. But very little time would pass before David would glance up to find Rebecca in the crowd and, smiling, return to the conversation.

Connor, looking uncomfortable but devastating nonetheless in black tie, prowled around the room making young and old feminine hearts flutter. Just generally being a Clayworth male, infinitely desirable because he seemed so very unattainable.

But her Clayworth male was within reach.

Athena lifted her head to look into Drew's eyes and saw the wealth of love, tenderness, and desire there.

Yes, together we can, will, overcome whatever life deals us.

He smiled down and pressed a kiss on her nose.

Maybe her high emotion made her more in tune with others.

Her father still seemed uncomfortable, and the problems he predicted for Clayworth's hadn't made their appearance yet, but she sensed they would. Whatever happened, she would be by Drew's side.

The way Connor and Venus so studiously ignored each other's existence seemed strangely powerful tonight.

Leaning into Drew, she felt his chest move in a deep chuckle. "For better or worse. They're family," he whispered into her ear, before gently biting it.

She twined their fingers together and raised his knuckles to her lips. "For better or worse. Always. I promise."

THE DISH

Where authors give you the inside scoop!

♥ ♥ ♥ ♥ ♥ ♥ ♥ ♥ ♥ ♥ ♥ ♥ ♥ ♥ ♥

From the desk of Susan Crandall

Dear Reader,

After a good friend of mine finished reading one of my suspense novels, she asked my husband how he could sleep next to me at night, knowing how my mind works. After I'd given her a good dose of stink-eye, I really started thinking. Not about how dangerous it is for my dear husband—although that could probably be debated. Many of us do it every night without pause, but think about how much trust it takes between two people to fall into innocent, blissful, and completely *defenseless* sleep next to that other person.

But more important to SLEEP NO MORE is the question: When in our lives are we more vulnerable than when we're sleeping? I mean, it starts when we're children with the monster in the closet or the bogeyman under the bed. And for sleepwalkers, that vulnerability multiplies exponentially; their fears are real and well-founded, not imaginary.

Think about it. You go to bed. Fall asleep... and never know what you might do during those sleeping hours. Eat everything in your refrigerator? Leave the house? Set a fire? It would be horrifying. Even worse, you will have absolutely no recollection of your actions.

As they say, "From tiny acorns mighty oaks do grow." The disturbing vulnerability induced by sleep-walking was the seed that grew into SLEEP NO MORE.

As for my husband... the poor man continues to slumber innocently next to me while my mind buzzes with things to keep the rest of you awake at night.

Please visit my Web site, www.susancrandall.net, for updates and extras you won't find between the covers.

Yours,

Susan Crandall

♥ ♥ ♥ ♥ ♥ ♥ ♥ ♥ ♥ ♥ ♥ ♥ ♥ ♥ ♥

From the desk of Sherrill Bodine

Darling Reader,

You know I can't resist sharing delicious secrets about some of Chicago's best stories!

When I discovered that my friend, the curator of costumes at the history museum, was poisoned by a black Dior evening gown (don't worry—he's perfectly well!) and that it happened at a top secret fall-out shelter that houses some of the most treasured gowns in Chicago's history, I knew I had to tell the tale in A BLACK TIE AFFAIR.

After all, what could be more irresistible than a

time-warp fantasy place that houses row after row of priceless gowns that were once worn by Bertha Palmer, the real-life legendary leader of Chicago's social scene?

For those of you who may not be familiar with her, Bertha leveraged her social standing and family fortune to improve lives and to champion women's rights. So I thought, how perfect it would be if her gowns helped the women of Chicago once again, and one woman in particular!

It wasn't long before my heroine, Athena Smith, was born. I gave her two fabulous sisters who are just as devoted to fashion as Athena is—and, of course, as I am—and I determined that a couture gown would change her life forever. One of Bertha's gowns would poison Athena, just as that Dior had poisoned my friend, and that would throw her back into the arms of her first love, notorious bachelor Drew Clayworth. Of course, that's just the tip of the iceberg of this story because, as we all know, the course of true love never does run smooth.

Find out what other surprises and tributes to my beloved Chicago I have in store for you in A BLACK TIE AFFAIR. And never forget that I love giving you a peek beneath society's glitter into its heart. Please tell me *your* secrets when you visit me at www.sherrill bodine.com.

XO

Sherrill Bodine

♥ ♥ ♥ ♥ ♥ ♥ ♥ ♥ ♥ ♥ ♥ ♥ ♥ ♥ ♥

From the desk of Amanda Scott

Dear Reader,

What sort of conflict between the heads of two powerful Scottish clans might have persuaded Robert Maxwell of Trailinghail to abduct Lady Mairi Dunwythie of Annandale, the heiress daughter of a baron who defied certain demands made by Maxwell that he believed were unwarranted? Next, having abducted the lady, what does Robert do when Lord Dunwythie still refuses to submit? And why on earth does Mairi, abducted and imprisoned by Robert, not only fall in love with him but later—long after she is safe and a powerful baroness in her own right—decide that she wants to marry him?

These are just a few of the challenging questions that faced me when I accepted an invitation to consider writing the "true" fourteenth-century story of Mairi Dunwythie and Robert Maxwell—now titled SEDUCED BY A ROGUE.

The invitation also came in the form of a question—a much simpler one: Would I be interested in the story of a woman who had nearly begun a clan war?

Since authors are always looking for new material, I promptly answered yes.

A friend had found an unpublished manuscript, dated April 16, 1544, and written in broad Scotch by

"Lady Maxwell." Broad Scotch is a language I do not know.

Fortunately, my friend does.

Lady Maxwell related details of how two fourteenth-century Dunwythie sisters met and married their husbands. ("Dunwythie" is the fourteenth-century spelling for Dinwiddie, Dunwoodie, and similar Scottish surnames.) SEDUCED BY A ROGUE is the story of the elder sister, Mairi.

Relying on details passed down in Maxwell anecdotes over a period of two hundred years, Lady Maxwell portrayed that clan favorably and Mairi's father as a scoundrel. The trouble, her ladyship wrote, was *all* Lord Dunwythie's fault.

So the challenge for me was to figure out the Dunwythies' side of things and what lay at the center of the conflict. That proved to be a fascinating puzzle.

Her ladyship provided few specifics, but the dispute clearly concerned land. The Maxwells thought they owned or controlled that land. Dunwythie disagreed.

The Maxwell who had claimed ownership (or threatened to *take* ownership) was just a Maxwell, not a lord or a knight. However, Dunwythie was *Lord* Dunwythie of Dunwythie, and that Annandale estate stayed in Dunwythie hands for nearly two hundred years longer. In the fourteenth century, landowners were knights, barons, or earls—or they were royal. So, clearly, Dunwythie owned the land.

Next, I discovered that the Maxwells were then the hereditary sheriffs of Dumfries. Sheriffs ("shire-reeves") were enormously powerful in both Scotland

and England, because they administered whole counties (shires), collected taxes, and held their own courts of law. The fact that Annandale lies within Dumfriesshire was a key to what most likely happened between the Dunwythies and the Maxwells.

The result is the trilogy that began with TAMED BY A LAIRD (January 2009) and continues now with SEDUCED BY A ROGUE. It will end with TEMPTED BY A WARRIOR (January 2010).

I hope you enjoy all of them. In the meantime, *Suas Alba!*

Amanda Scott

http://home.att.net/~amandascott
amandascott@worldnet.att.net